A Good Year
Unhallowed Love Series
Book 1

Tara Fox Hall

Published by
Melange Books, LLC
White Bear Lake, MN 55110
www.melange-books.com

"For Mom: my editor, perennial parent, and always friend"

Chapter One

"To another fabulous year at Pandora Productions!" Mrs. Rebecca Pall said cheerily, flashing a red-lipped smile at her employees. Her husband Paul raised his glass, his expression slightly less enthusiastic.

If you only knew, Debbie thought, clapping with the others at her sides, the fake smile plastered on her face slipping the slightest fraction. *You're about to lose your company, along with your husband.*

She had had to arrange it, of course. Paul hadn't the guts to kill. His thrilling attributes were few and far between. Their affair hadn't been one of lust, at least on Debbie's part. Paul's assets were what she lusted for: the multi-million dollar company called Pandora Productions that she had given her life to help build.

True, the idea of the film production company had been Rebecca's, back when they were both students in business school and eager to make their mark on the world. Debbie had been reluctant, knowing how hard it was to launch a business in a normal economy, much less a recession. But Rebecca had been insistent that if they focused on quality content, superb editing, and cutting edge special effects, Pandora Productions could become not only a reality, but an ultra-successful one. Caught in the enthusiasm and drive of her new friend, Debbie had signed on. It was Debbie herself who in her zeal for mythology and legends had come up with the name Pandora Productions.

Rebecca had that gift, that charisma to draw people to her causes. With a few bright techs and film students. Pandora Productions had become a reality. Just a campus organization at first, it quickly became renowned for excellent short films. Then, in sophomore year, their short film about discrimination won second place at the Sundance Film Festival. More prestigious awards followed, as the films became longer and better, the result of investing in top-of-the-line equipment and more talent flocking to the Pandora name. Finally, with the epic fantasy *Blue Daylight*, Pandora Productions had won the coveted Gotham Award, the most prestigious American award available for independent films.

It hadn't been a glamorous ascent, but the result of hours and years of hard work, skipped meals, all-nighters, and hard decisions. Rebecca and Debbie had been together through it all, side by side, the best of friends.

Then had come Paul Pall, a handsome film student five years younger than Debbie and Rebecca and eager to make his mark on the world. As his name suggested, he had cast a shadow not only on the company, but also on Debbie and Rebecca's friendship.

Debbie had known that the insufferable Paul had his sights on the company she had slaved for, that all it represented to him was an easy future. She avoided him, and advised Rebecca to do the same. But her friend that had for years seen every pitfall and shyster for what they were was suddenly blind. Worse, Rebecca had turned against Debbie, accusing her of jealousy.

Debbie had thought about leaving, and starting over. She had the skills and the contacts. But why should she, after all the years she had put into Pandora? A decade had passed. The unrelenting work of building up a business that had been fine in her early twenties wasn't something she was eager to repeat. No, Paul had to go.

But what about Rebecca? Debbie hated to throw away her friendship after all they had struggled through together. So Debbie made plans for Paul alone, deciding once he was gone that Rebecca would become the friend she used to be, especially with Debbie's staunch shoulder to cry on. Murder was out; there was too much risk. No, what better way to show Paul for the villain he was than to seduce him, then expose the affair to Rebecca in a tearful confession?

Enduring Paul's touch had been the hardest part of Debbie's plan. Thankfully, the man was a ten minute wonder, and not at all concerned with her satisfaction. After a month of sordid couplings, Debbie readied herself for a confession just before Christmas, when she thought it would have the most effect. It was also the most her conscience would stand for. She had never kept anything from Rebecca before now, and the guilt and shame of being with her best friend's husband was unbearable.

Then had come the surprise meeting a week ago, Paul looking on while Rebecca told her that they had decided to sell their shares of Pandora to one of the Hollywood film conglomerates, Titan Pictures.

Debbie had been stunned. "But…they'll dissolve Pandora!"

"No," Rebecca had assured her. "We've made sure that Pandora will survive, and you're not going anywhere, either, Debbie. You'll head up the company. I'm signing papers January 2nd to attest to that."

"Rebecca would have signed them already," Paul put in. "But she was looking out for you, Debbie. She made them stipulate that your job as CEO of Pandora was non-negotiable." He winked at Debbie.

He likely told her to cut me loose. Bastard, Debbie thought.

"Everything will be the same," Rebecca continued. "Except that you'll be running Pandora on your own. Titan plans to reduce the workforce, but that's the only change. They want Pandora to focus more on independent films—"

And Titan will call all the shots, Debbie thought darkly. *I'll be nothing more than a figurehead.* "Are you retiring?"

"We need to focus on having a family," Paul said, putting his hand over Rebecca's. "With her hectic schedule here at Pandora, Rebecca hasn't been able to relax enough."

"I can take on more work," Debbie said quickly, seeing a glimmer of hope. "If you'd only said something, Becky—"

"Deb, I haven't been able to conceive," Rebecca said harshly, strain etching her face. "It's been close to two years, and nothing. I want to have a family before it's too late."

Debbie blinked, stunned. Rebecca had never mentioned getting pregnant to her at all, or even wanting to have children. *How had they drifted so far apart?* "I didn't know."

"Take the job," Paul said, offering her a meaningful smile. "You've made Pandora a success, Debbie. It's time you took a break too, and enjoyed life." He kissed Rebecca's cheek. "We're going to. We've had a long talk about recommitting to one another."

Paul had confessed an affair, just not with her, and in that action, nullified her plan. Her shame of the past month had been for absolutely nothing. Debbie settled her face into neutral with effort, seething with frustrated anger.

"I'm going to announce you as the new head of operations on the first day of the New Year," Rebecca said, shouldering her purse. "You and I will also sit down with Titan that morning to talk about transitioning my duties to you. But please don't let anyone else know yet, okay? This was Pandora's best year yet. I want Pandora's New Year's Eve party to focus on that." Rebecca smiled. "Have a merry Christmas, Debbie."

Debbie nodded. "I won't. Merry Christmas."

Rebecca and Paul had exited, leaving Debbie to stew in thoughts of vengeance, wounded betrayal, and indecision. Many possible actions filled her mind for the next hour, as she tried to think of what to do. But no scenario she thought up brought Rebecca back to her and got rid of Paul.

"God damn him!" she shouted finally, shoving the top of her desk's contents to the floor. "Damn him to Hell!"

"A common wish this time of the year," said a sulfurous voice.

Debbie blinked. Out of the shadows stepped a monstrous creature, a demon from the dark ages. His upper torso was bare, his skin flushed red, straight black hair in a short ponytail. His lower body was animal: dark brown fur and black cloven hooves. A loincloth swathed his hips, made of some kind of tanned leather.

"What are you?" Debbie said, unafraid. "Some kind of method actor? Auditions have been closed for *Hell's Gate* since Tuesday."

The thing chuckled. "No, I've no interest in being in pictures. But this is an audition of sorts, yes." The thing moved closer. "Didn't you say you wanted Paul in Hell? Or did I misunderstand you?"

"Get out," Debbie said, kneeling to gather up scattered paper and pens from the floor. "I've no time for your bullshit."

The thing dropped to its haunches, then grabbed her left arm with its hand. "I'm no concoction of man's making, human."

Debbie screamed, the heat of the thing's touch blistering her skin. She pulled backward, sprawling on her ass on the floor, a handprint of reddened skin on her forearm.

The thing stood, then offered its hand, each finger tipped with a shiny black claw. Debbie took a deep breath, then grasped the proffered limb, the heat now that of normal human flesh. She examined it carefully, looking for the telltale signs of makeup, prosthetics, or other fakery. There were none.

"You're real," she said shakily, standing on her own.

"If you are done inspecting me," the demon uttered, "we can get to business, hopefully."

"You want my soul," Debbie stated. "In return for taking care of Paul, I'd gladly give it."

"Not really," the demon said in an offhand manner. "I want a favor from you, to be determined later. In exchange, I'll take care of Paul."

"How?" Debbie said.

The demon held out his hand again. This time, it held a bottle, the label ornate and handwritten. "There will be a party on New Year's, or so your friend mentioned. Serve this to them."

"I don't want Rebecca hurt," Debbie replied.

"Paul will be the only one affected," the demon assured. "I will protect you. Once he is stricken, I'll take it from there."

Debbie nodded, then took the proffered bottle. "Agreed. What do I call you?"

"Shaker," the demon said its smile of shark's teeth chilling. "Good doing business with you, Deb."

Another round of boisterous clapping jolted Debbie out of her memories. She forced a smile on her face, as Rebecca and Paul threaded their way through the crowd to her.

"I'm so glad the speech came off well," Paul said happily. "Knowing it's the last one I'll ever have to make is such a relief."

"Shh," Rebecca chided. She turned to Debbie. "Do you have a moment? I wanted to give you a little something."

"Yes," Debbie said eagerly. "I have something for you and Paul, too. Let's go into my office."

The three slipped away from the other partygoers down the hall to Debbie's office. Carefully, Debbie unstopped the bottle, and poured three glasses. "A toast," Debbie said, raising her glass. "To Pandora, and to us, who have worked our asses off, and now will reap the rewards."

The three clinked glasses, then sipped the wine. "A strange taste," Paul said, looking at the label quizzically. "I really like it, though. Where did you find it?"

"A new friend," Debbie said, smiling. "He said it was a good year."

"From us," Rebecca said, offering Debbie a small wrapped box.

Debbie put down her glass and opened the box. It was a small chest, engraved in winged creatures. She opened it, to reveal a small charm bracelet made of gold and pearls. "Thank you," Debbie said, a stab of guilt making her flush.

Rebecca took out the bracelet, and began fastening it on Debbie's wrist. "So tell us all about your new friend, Debbie. You never mentioned him—"

Paul bellowed, then went to his knees, his face flushing, eyes wild as blood ran from his temples where black prongs were erupting. Debbie and Rebecca screamed, then moved backwards from the flailing man.

"Paul!" Rebecca shouted, starting for her husband. "No," Debbie said, grabbing hold of her friend. "He'll hurt you!"

Paul convulsed, his body rippling, becoming more powerful as clothing ripped, revealing reddening flesh and growing muscles. His lower torso began undulating, becoming reptilian as scales formed and claws burst outwards from his shiny Brooks Brothers shoes.

"Paul!" Rebecca screeched, fighting free of Debbie. She flung herself toward Paul, reaching toward his hands to hold him down. Paul flailed, his taloned hand connecting with Rebecca. She fell backward, her skull caving slightly as it smashed into the edge of Debbie's desk.

"No!" Debbie yelled, hurrying to her friend. She pulled with all her strength on Rebecca's prone form, dragging her away from Paul.

"What…have you done…to me?" Paul rasped out, his red eyes focusing on Debbie. "You…bitch—" He darted for her on all fours, claws raking the floor.

Shaker appeared, grasping Paul by the nape of his now scaly neck. "Not a chance." With a smile at Debbie, he and Paul disappeared.

Debbie sighed in relief, then reluctantly left Rebecca's side, calling for help.

* * * *

Three hours later, Debbie entered her penthouse apartment, breathing a second relieved sigh as she tossed her keys on the end table, and kicked off her high heels.

Everything had gone better than she'd hoped. Rebecca was okay, the knock on the head serious but not fatal. She'd awoken raving about Paul becoming a beast in the middle of the ambulance ride to the hospital, and the EMT's had sedated her. She'd be released tomorrow, most likely.

Debbie had spun a vague story about Paul going crazy, hitting Becky, then running out of the room. Even now, the police were looking for him. He'd be no more trouble. Without him, Becky would be her old self.

A sharp pain minced through Debbie's fingers of her left hand. She flexed her digits, then went back to her musings.

Becky would have to go along with Debbie's story. What was she going to say, that Paul had transformed into a monster before her eyes? No one would believe her, even if she did try to tell the truth. Worst-case scenario, Becky would be admitted to a mental hospital for a while, and Debbie would take Pandora's reins. The deal with Titan would fall through, no matter what. That was what mattered.

Another sharp pain lanced along Debbie's right hand, then down her index finger. She flexed that hand, then took out the small box Becky had gifted to her. Opening it, Debbie looked again at the bracelet that Becky had given to her. Pearls were her favorite. She fastened it on her wrist, then headed to the bathroom to see how the bracelet sparkled in bright light.

At her second step, burning pain lanced around her left ankle, then travelled upward in a spiral. Debbie shrieked, then went to one knee, her skin crawling with movement, a hundred pricks of fire lancing pain down into her skin. She staggered to the mirror and looked, then shrieked again.

Waspy winged things crawled all over her, stinging her as she watched. Several were emerging out of her skin, shaking off bloody wings. Others were laying eggs in her, leaving pulsating welts behind in rows as larva birthed and gorged itself. As she opened her mouth to scream, Debbie saw two smaller creatures buzzing happily, as they crawled into her mouth, even as a large one squeezed itself out her nose. With a thud, Debbie collapsed in a faint.

"Wake up, human."

Debbie blinked her eyes, then remembered the bugs on her. She let out a scream, brushing at herself.

"They're gone," Shaker intoned from her easy chair, bemused.

"What were they?" Debbie said, shivering as she scanned her mirror image for signs of the bugs.

"Demons call them Invisible Stings," Shaker replied. "An excruciating way to die, if you don't go mad first." He held out the gift box to her. "Don't you know better than to open boxes?"

Debbie's face contorted in fury, then she ripped at the bracelet that circled her wrist. "That bastard!"

"No. Your friend, Rebecca," Shaker said, crushing the box into a misshapen metal lump. "I did a little investigating, while you were unconscious. You're just lucky that you had a stronger ally in your vengeance that she did."

"Why?" Debbie said, horrified.

"You slept with Paul, her husband," Shaker said. "At least, that was the reason the witch who supplied her with the curse gave before I killed her."

Debbie rubbed at her skin. *What would she do now? Rebecca had betrayed her.* "Thanks for saving me."

"Just protecting my investment," Shaker said pleasantly. "Though I guess you could say you owe me two favors now."

"Make it three," Debbie said, meeting his red gaze with her resolute one. "Make sure that Becky stays out of my way. But don't kill her. She might have wanted to kill me, but we were friends once."

"Thy will be done," Shaker said formally, then laughed. "I'm sure Pandora Productions will flourish under your rule." He produced a bottle of wine, this one with a familiar label. "I know you like reds. Shall we drink to it?"

Debbie glanced at the clock. In a few minutes, the New Year would arrive. "Yes," she said with determination. "To the best damn year ever. Pour, demon."

Chapter Two

~ January ~

Debbie looked up from the haphazard pile of papers on the desk in front of her to the clock. Damn, it was already seven. She'd wanted to be home an hour ago.

She pushed the papers away, then rubbed her sore eyes. Where were the damn drops the doctor had prescribed? She couldn't afford blurry vision now.

A clawed hand rested on her shoulder, the sheer heat of the reddish skin against hers instantly soothing. "You should go home, Mistress."

Debbie leaned back her head, smiling tiredly at the demon looming over her. "I can't, Shaker. I went through too much to get control of Pandora's reins to let everything go to Hell."

Shaker rubbed her shoulders. Debbie smiled and closed her eyes, the soothing hotness of his touch unknotting her aching muscles.

"So what is it tonight?" Shaker intoned. "Piracy issues, copyrights, or both?"

"That, some governmental red tape, distribution, international markets, and tack on increased fees," Debbie replied, stifling a yawn with her hand. "You name the problem, and I've got it. I feel like every enemy I've ever had has come out of the woodwork."

"Including Paul's son?"

Debbie grimaced. "If I'd known that bastard gave a damn about his father, I would have told you to kill him, too. Dante called me again today, yelling about how he knew I'd had his father abducted. He's threatening to sue me."

"He can prove nothing," Shaker soothed, still kneading Debbie's shoulders. "There is no evidence that anything happened to Paul."

"But there is also no evidence that he's alive and well someplace, either," Debbie countered sourly. "I don't suppose you can change your form and pretend to be him in some other country for a while?"

"I could arrange something," Shaker said after a moment, pausing in his massaging. "But Paul's son is not really interested in his father. He's interested in the inheritance he thinks he's missing out on. You said that Paul has been declared missing, but not dead. Dante cares less about punishing you than claiming his father's share of the company."

"Becky's share," Debbie said sadly. She blinked rapidly, her eyes already filling.

"It wasn't your fault she took her own life," Shaker whispered, resuming his kneading. "She was already unstable, because of Paul's relentless machinations. He made her feel inadequate and insecure to the point she believed she couldn't handle living without him. Then when he died, she broke."

He said it as if Rebecca were a toy, not a person. "How can you know that?" Debbie murmured, wanting to be soothed.

"I don't," Shaker replied with a chuckle. "But after a thousand years, I've got a good handle on human motivations."

Debbie's eyes snapped open, and she half turned in her chair to look at Shaker. "You're that old?"

He smiled, showing his shark-like teeth. "Technically older, but that's all I'm admitting to."

"Fair enough," Debbie said. "Thanks for the massage. I should get back to work."

"On the contrary," Shaker said. "I'm taking you home." He leaned over in a graceful motion, gathering up a protesting Debbie from her office chair. In a blink, Shaker was standing in Debbie's living room.

"What the hell?" Debbie exclaimed.

"Teleportation, of course," Shaker said, going to the liquor cabinet. He brought out a bottle of 10-year Ardbeg, and poured two shots. Taking up both glasses, he brought one to her. "Sit down and have a drink,

Mistress."

Debbie was too tired to protest. She kicked off her heels, then sat back into her easy chair, sipping the alcohol. At first, she had been loath to try scotch. But at Shaker's insistence, she had developed a taste for it.

Debbie looked over again at her demon. God, it was still odd to think of him that way, even if she was getting used to his horns and cloven feet. Maybe it was because he'd never asked for her soul, or acted like the demons in movies. Or it could have been his manner, which was always slightly teasing, yet polite and well spoken. Shaker had a good sense of humor, a quality Debbie had appreciated more and more in the opposite sex, as she grew older. *If only more of the men her own age were like him...*

"You're staring at me," Shaker said with a smile. "Ready to take our relationship to the next level?"

In a flash, Debbie's calm, peaceful attitude was gone. Her eyes bugged out, and she nearly dropped her drink. "Excuse me?"

"You know exactly what I meant, Mistress," Shaker said with a laugh. "But as the answer is clearly no, I'll move on to business." He drained his shot in one swallow, then set down the empty glass. "I can help with your problems, Mistress. Dante will be the top priority clearly, but you will have to give me some facts and figures on the other problems in the coming months. I need as much information as you can give me in the simplest format."

Debbie blinked. "Then in my simplest terms: what the hell does that mean, Shaker? I could give you a five-foot stack of paperwork on the copyright issues alone."

"I need you to look over each situation and find the base problem," Shaker replied. "Then give me your preferred way to solve it." He grinned, again baring his shark-like rows of teeth. "I can come up with solutions myself, of course, but I do not have your ethics. And I would not want to upset you so early in our relationship, my gentle human. So I'd like your suggestions to think over before I act on my own."

Debbie resisted the urge to bolt her scotch, her heart hammering in her chest. "I can get you that, no problem. But what about Dante?"

"Let me look into the matter, and I'll meet you here tomorrow night," Shaker said. He disappeared.

Debbie eased herself back into her chair, forcing herself to take long deep breaths. She was in control of this situation. She just had to make sure that the status quo didn't change.

* * * *

"You create the scenes and conditions for movies. I don't see why the deal can't go through, Debbie."

"That's Ms. Deal," Debbie corrected scathingly, glaring at the Titan Pictures representative. "I handle all the production decisions at Pandora. My team and I initiate, co-ordinate, supervise and control everything from fund-raising to hiring key personnel to arranging for distributors." Her tone turned icy to drive the point home. "In other words, I have ultimate creative control, something your contract neglects to mention."

"Let me be to the point, since you're being so frank," the executive said, his tone now hostile. "Titan wants Pandora, with you or without you. Make it easy, and you stand to get most of the perks that Rebecca detailed out. Fight us, and you'll not only be out of a job, Ms. Deal, but you'll also be blacklisted."

"Get out," Debbie growled. "Now."

The executive gave her a shake of his head coupled with a sorrowful look, then sauntered out of her office. Debbie gritted her teeth, her hands clenched into fists in her lap.

Her secretary Amanda came in. "Your 10 o'clock is here. Do you want me to have him wait for a while?"

God, it had taken all her will not to bean that bastard with her office plant. "No, Amanda," Debbie said with a sigh. "Show him in."

"If you don't mind me asking, Debbie, what's the word?" Amanda asked. "We all heard about the proposed announcement at the New Year's party, but then Paul disappeared and Rebecca—"

"I don't want to sell to Titan," Debbie admitted. "I'm not going through with it. They aren't pleased, which is why that prick keeps coming back here each week."

"Why not?" Amanda asked. "Not that I want to look for a new job, but you could make out like a bandit."

"Because money isn't everything," Debbie said staunchly. "I love what I do, Amanda. I am not giving that up."

Amanda nodded and smiled, yet it was in her blank gaze that she didn't understand. "I'll show in Mr. Triss."

Debbie looked through her papers, then brought out Mr. Triss's resume. The man may have had a girly-sounding name, but there was nothing girly about his accomplishments. If he'd done even half of what he claimed, he'd be an asset she could make good use of. The only thing odd on his resume was that he had no first name listed at all, not even an initial.

The door opened, and a lithe man stepped inside, his suit of grey wool looking so new he might have bought it right before the interview.

"Please sit down, Mr. Triss," Debbie said, indicating the empty chair opposite her desk.

The man smiled, and sat down easily, leaning back and staring at her. Debbie stared back at him, unnerved but also intrigued at his blatant confidence.

"Do you want me to start the interview?" Mr. Triss said finally. "I'm happy to expound on my qualifications."

"Tell me your first name, Mr. Triss."

The man smiled uncomfortably. "I'd prefer to go just by my last name, if that's okay."

"That's fine," Debbie replied. "But I want to know it to satisfy my curiosity."

"Rack," the man said, shifting uncomfortably. "But I must stipulate that you not call me that if I'm hired."

God, he was odd. Debbie was already sure she wasn't going to hire him, but the last thing she wanted was to antagonize a potential maniac. "Agreed. Please tell me a little about yourself, Mr. Triss."

For the next half hour, Debbie asked various questions and Rack answered them. His attitude was polite, and his replies precise and knowledgeable. When she gave him the usual "we'll call you" speech, he just gave her a wink, and smiled. She breathed a sigh of relief, then told Amanda to show in the next candidate.

At the close of the day, Debbie rubbed her eyes and looked over the interviewees. Mr. Triss—aka Rack—was the clear choice for her new acquisitions manager. Yet there was something unnerving about him, reminding her of someone who'd wronged her years ago. And that was besides all that weirdness about him not giving her his first name. She'd go with the second name on the list, a woman named Sheila Bernard. Maybe she hadn't had all the experience that Mr. Triss had, but her behavior had raised no red flags.

* * * *

The last day of January, Debbie took Sheila out to lunch at Andy's. It was an upscale restaurant that had the benefit of actually serving delectable food, something Debbie admitted to herself was not a usual occurrence in fine dining.

As they looked over the menus, Sheila sighed, then put her menu down. "It's the same choice as always, really. Do I enjoy myself or hold to the diet?" She chuckled, then stifled it when several older patrons in formal dress looked their way with disdainful expressions.

Debbie smiled widely, even as she bit her lip to hold in her own laughter. It was hard not to laugh with Sheila. Even though they'd known each other less than a month, they'd become fast friends. Some of that was Sheila's personality; vibrant, optimistic, outspokenly forthright, and easy to joke with. The rest was her work ethic and zeal for Pandora, which matched Debbie's own.

"What do you think?" Sheila asked with a smirk. "Diet or fun? I think we could use a little fun."

"We could indeed," Debbie said with a raise of her brows. "We've been working our asses off." Her expression turned serious. "Which is why I wanted to take you to lunch, Sheila. I want you to know that I appreciate your great work so far on Pandora. You may not have been there long, but you've done a fabulous job helping get us back on track."

"I appreciate that," Sheila replied seriously, her grin fading. "I really like working at Pandora, and with you. But I have to admit that these last few weeks I seem to be on a lucky streak, so I'm not sure I can take all the credit."

"You've worked your butt off," Debbie reaffirmed, "which is why I'm giving you the rest of the afternoon off." She motioned to the waiter, who brought over a bottle of wine and two glasses. "Your acquisition of those last two pictures was brilliant."

Sheila shook her head, a familiar expression of obstinacy gracing her features. "That's really thoughtful of you, Debbie, but I'm serious. I've gotten no resistance to any action I've taken on Pandora's behalf, something I've never experienced before in this business…hell, any business! You're right that those pictures were brilliant, and we got them for a great price. But why were there no other bidders? I admit I'm fabulous, but I'm not the only stellar buyer around."

The waiter had already poured the wine. Debbie picked up her glass and raised it. "You helped me and Pandora over a rough patch. Genius or not, you deserve recognition. Now take a sip at least, since I've already paid for it."

Sheila smiled good-naturedly, raised her glass, and clinked it against Debbie's. "To more months with no issues, my excellent co-worker."

They both sipped silently, then Sheila went back to perusing the menu. Debbie was silent, her thoughts racing. Sheila's confession was likely the truth.

Sheila's right in that since she came on board, we've been blessed. Titan has stopped sending reps, even if they haven't given up completely. Dante also hadn't been heard from; last she'd heard he was busy dealing with Paul's other business, a promotional item corporation that had faltered and filed for bankruptcy the first of the year. The other issues she'd mentioned to Shaker hadn't gone away, really, but they'd become manageable, compromises struck so that Pandora could not only finish up its various films in progress, it could also procure new ones with merit. Did Shaker have something to do with it?

"I'm going to be bad, I think," Sheila said with glee. "I think the fettuccini alfredo. Want to be evil with me?"

Debbie glanced over at Sheila. *Did Shaker have something to do with Sheila?*

Sheila glanced up, her brow wrinkling instantly at Debbie's odd expression. "What?"

Debbie forced a smile. "Nothing. I'm just tired."

"Because you've been working your butt off too, my dear," Sheila said. "Which means if you are making me take the rest of the day off, then you are, too."

Debbie immediately began to protest. "I'm the president, I can't just leave—"

A Good Year

"Things are not going to fall apart if you play hooky one afternoon," Sheila pronounced. "Besides, woman to woman, you need a break, Debbie. We have been on a gold streak lately, and it's sure to end at some point. That's just how business is. So take some time off and enjoy it. We'll have a fight on our hands soon enough."

Knowing her friend was right, Debbie nodded. It wouldn't hurt to take one afternoon off. She would leave her cell on. If there was some emergency, she could always go back in.

"To a long afternoon of relaxing," Sheila said, raising her glass. "Why don't we hit the spa? The Black Rose is right near the shopping mall, and we can do a little buying before we head home." She smiled. "Now are you going to be bad or not?"

"Yes," Debbie answered with a wicked grin. "Let's be very bad."

* * * *

Stuffed to the gills, Debbie followed Sheila to the spa in her car. The building was a non-descript brick structure with little landscaping. A huge picture of a glistening black rose graced the large front window of the shop. *The Black Rose* was written in silver underneath, the gothic letters glittering in the sharp winter sunlight.

"Have you ever been here?" Debbie whispered to Sheila as they entered.

"No," Sheila whispered back. "But I've driven by a lot of times and wanted to come in and find out what they offer. Have you?"

"I've never had time," Debbie admitted, conscious of her hands that were bare of nail polish and her simple hairstyle. She shifted her feet awkwardly as she stood at the counter near Sheila. *What would they say when they looked at her feet?* Debbie had never had a pedicure in her life.

"Good afternoon, ladies," a young woman said brightly, striding up. "Do you have an appointment?"

"No," Sheila answered with a smile. "But we'd like one for whatever you can do on a walk in basis. My friend and I always wanted to try this shop, and suddenly had a free afternoon." She winked at the girl.

The woman looked apologetic, her expression so remorseful that

21

Debbie's trained eye easily recognized the falseness of bad acting. "I'm sorry. We don't do walk-ins. But I'm happy to make an appointment for both of you for another day. We have a deal for first time—"

"There are only our cars in your parking lot out front," Sheila said heatedly, her irritation making a flush rise in her cheeks. "We're happy to pay full price, but we want service today." Her smile had become a shark's grin. "You don't want to ruin our day, do you?"

"I'm sorry," the girl said politely. "But we don't do walk-ins. I must insist you make an appointment."

Sheila was beet red, madder than Debbie had ever seen her. Whether she was going to make a scene or not, this wasn't worth it. "Let's go," Debbie said, touching Sheila's arm. She gave the girl a cool look. "They don't want our business today."

"Any business," sneered Sheila. "Don't worry, honey, we'll spread the word."

Debbie and Sheila turned for the exit, walking quickly. "Maybe it's a sign," Debbie said lightly, trying to get Sheila to smile. "Pandora likely needs us—"

"Pandora Pictures?" the girl exclaimed from behind them. She came out from behind the counter like a shot, her heels clacking. "I'm so sorry. I didn't know!"

Debbie and Sheila turned, incredulous. "Excuse me?" Sheila said snottily.

The girl's expression was unmistakably horrified. Yet as Debbie watched, her face smoothed back into its smile, albeit slightly lopsided. "We received a call back around Christmas," she said. "Are you Debbie Deal?"

"Yes," Debbie answered, giving a shrug to a curious Sheila.

"You were gifted with a year's worth of monthly visits, Ms. Deal," the girl said. "I am so sorry. I'd never seen you, so I didn't recognize you."

That uneasy feeling was back in full force. Who would have bought her time at Black Rose? "But I still don't have an appointment," Debbie said blatantly. "Doesn't that matter?"

"No," the girl assured her. "This was already paid for. With gifts of that kind—"

"That size," Sheila said under her breath.

"—we don't require an appointment, at least for the first visit," the girl finished. "But appointments are appreciated for all visits, yes." She beckoned to Debbie, heading back to the counter. "What did you have in mind for today, Ms. Deal?"

"How much does the gift certificate allow for?" Debbie asked curiously, following her with Sheila in tow. "Can I give one of the months to my friend to enjoy with me today?"

Sheila looked pleased, but also unsure if she should accept.

The girl nodded. "Of course you can share. And as for the gift's monthly allowance, the certificate is for half a day's worth of procedures each month. That includes an hour body wrap, full manicure with nails and polish, pedicure, facial, haircut, and an hour massage."

That sounded like a full day, Debbie thought happily. "Do I have to take all the procedures? I have my own hairstylist."

"No," the girl said. "You can exchange for procedures of equal value. The pedicure and the full manicure are equal. The massage and the wrap are about equal. And the haircut and the facial are also the same."

Debbie turned to Sheila. "This was your idea. And no arguing on my treating. Thoughts?"

Sheila nodded. "Let's each have the facial, the manicure and the wrap." She looked back at the girl. "Is that doable?"

"Yes, we keep one person on staff at all times," the girl assured. "And I'm a provider as well as the day manager. Follow me."

She led them into the back of the shop, calling softly, "Eduardo!" As they approached a hallway of doors, a solemn young man dressed in black appeared from the second room, his dour expression breaking into a smile at the sight of Debbie and Sheila.

"Wrap, facial and manicure," the girl said to him, gesturing to Sheila. She followed Eduardo into the room, casting a single devilish grin at Debbie before the door shut.

"Follow me," the girl said brightly to Debbie, heading to the third door.

Why couldn't she have gotten the hot guy instead of the pretty girl? Debbie sighed, then followed the girl into the room.

"I'm Vivian," the girl said as she shut the door behind them, flushing. "Sorry I didn't say so before. I was just so embarrassed." Again, she gave the fake sorrowful look, but under it, Debbie glimpsed a trace of Vivian's former horror. "Please undress to your underwear."

"I don't see how you could recognize someone you'd never met," Debbie said slowly, trying to decide if she wanted to undress in front of a woman half her age. *Of all the days to wear her oldest pair of underwear. And of course her bra didn't match it at all.* "Are there different wraps to choose from? This is my first time, but—"

Vivian flushed again, her mortification this time real. "Yes. Sorry. There is a lavender one, a seaweed one, and a mud one. Which one would you prefer?"

"Lavender, please."

Debbie spent the next hour luxuriating in the hot towels, feeling Vivian massage her body part by part with warm lavender oils. It was heavenly. Best of all, even after she was dressed, she could still smell the wonderful scented oil on her skin.

The facial was just as nice, though one of the lotions that Vivian applied burned a bit. But Debbie couldn't argue that the pinching feeling wasn't worth the results. Her face felt much softer and supple after the treatments. She emerged to join Sheila in another room equipped with tables and all kinds of polish. There Vivian proceeded to torture her hands with something that looked like a pointed trowel, pushing the skin at the bottom of each nail as far as it would go. Debbie grimaced, too proud to admit this was her first manicure. And she did like the look of Vivian's hands, with the pink of her nails long under the clear polish.

Too soon, Vivian was applying the polish topcoat, and then she and Eduardo left Sheila and Debbie under the small fans to dry.

"This was fun," Sheila said happily. She closed her eyes, leaning back in her chair and wiggling her drying fingers. "This is the life."

"You're just saying that because you got Eduardo," Debbie teased. "I'm going with him next time. You can have Vivian."

"He's all yours," Sheila said. "He didn't say anything to me except to ask what wrap to get. But his hands were very skilled—"

Debbie laughed. "Which one did you get?"

"Lavender. That seemed the best of the options, though the seaweed one I would like to try. Who wants to be smeared with mud? I could do that myself with some dirt."

"Maybe it's scented mud," Debbie said absently.

"In any case I'm glad we tried this," Sheila said. "I'll be happy to come with you next month, but I'm paying for my own, of course." She glanced over at Debbie. "Did you find out who gave you this awesome present?"

"No," Debbie said curiously. "But I intend to."

When their nails were dry, both women walked out to the counter where Vivian waited. They booked an appointment for the same time next month, and Vivian gave them a small card with the time, date, and a black rose on it.

"There's no number?" Sheila said. "What if we have to cancel?"

"Rare, but it does happen," Vivian said breezily, her tenseness gone. "It's on the back, Ma'am."

"Thank you," Debbie said. "If you could do one more thing for me, Vivian, I'd appreciate it. Who gave me this wonderful gift? I'd like to thank them in person."

Vivian smiled. "We can't give out this info. I'd guess it was your boyfriend, Ms. Deal."

Debbie's eyes narrowed. "I don't have a boyfriend, Vivian. Now give me that information."

Vivian shrugged, then went to her appointment book, flipping back several pages. "I'm sorry," she said after a moment, fake sorrow once more etched on her features. "I only have your name, the amount, and the credit card number we billed to."

"An unknown admirer," Sheila teased. "Sweet!"

"Don't you even have a phone number?" Debbie persisted.

Vivian shook her head. "We do have the name of Pandora pictures, but that's something I added." She looked up. "We often have husbands gift packages to their wives, and the wives usually come in right away in the first week to schedule their first visit. When I didn't hear from you in a couple weeks, I mentioned it to my boss, and he said you worked for Pandora. I looked up the office phone myself." She looked up from the book, smiling widely. "I'm so glad that you happened to come in today. It's wonderful to surprise a client with good news."

Vivian was clearly lying about the gift, but Debbie obviously wasn't going to get the real story out of her. "Thank you," she said, then left.

Sheila followed her out, grinning. "This is so cool, Debbie. The guy must have megabucks to do this for you."

"But it bothers me I don't know who he is," Debbie muttered, getting into her car.

"My advice?" Sheila said gleefully. "Just give it a month or so. He'll come to you."

"On Valentine's Day?" Debbie said flatly. "Wouldn't it make sense my white knight would send me a card telling me about his spectacular gift before today, instead of giving me the gift out of the blue with no warning?"

"Maybe VDay is too much pressure for him," Sheila offered. "Maybe he's waiting for another day special to him to contact you. Guys don't give expensive presents like these without wanting credit for it. He's probably just waiting for you to enjoy yourself before admitting he did it. Or maybe he's abnormally shy." She paused, staring at Debbie. "Are you sure you don't have anyone interested in you?"

Only a demon, Debbie thought.

Chaper Three

~ February ~

"You're a bully and a bitch!" a shrill voice proclaimed.

Debbie swore under her breath, got up from her desk, and ran through her open office door. More yelling was coming from down the hallway.

"I told you, you're fired! Now please leave!"

"I'm not leaving without talking to Debbie!"

Debbie entered the office. Amanda was there with Sheila and Giorgio, head of Pandora's legal department. They were facing off against Manny, former head of distribution and marketing. The last turned gratefully to her as she appeared, opening his mouth at once.

"No," Debbie said to Manny before he could start. "In my office. Sheila, please come too."

The three of them trooped back to Debbie's office, Manny and Sheila sitting down in chairs as Debbie sat down at her desk.

Manny began talking at once. "Sheila doesn't have the right to fire me—"

"Manny," Debbie said as patiently as she could. "We've been over this. Sheila is now my VP, as well as acquisitions manager for Pandora. She had authority to fire you. Furthermore, she did so on my say-so."

"I've been a loyal employee for the last decade—"

"In point of fact you haven't," Sheila interrupted. "Which is why I fired you. Your job entails that you get us the best deal for the widest distribution at the most profit. Instead, you were giving deals to your brother's marketing company that included exclusivity. I'd wondered why sales of *Tinderbox* were practically non-existent, even with all the ads I booked. He'd marked up the cost so much that only a few theaters booked runs at all." She turned to Debbie. "Fixed now, with a little added footage into an extended version at little additional cost to us, Deb. But the ads for the last month I can't do anything about. That money was wasted."

"I was the one that got the lead for *Tinderbox*," Manny persisted. "Saul Stevens would never have signed if it hadn't have been for all my work—"

"You mean your bribe, which cost the company heavily," Sheila said snidely. "Saul is not a rising star, he's a falling one. It was Jeremy's finding Carolina Andrun for flames and scenery that made that picture, and my own new star, Jett Black, that made *Tinderbox* have sex appeal. Which is why I got my promotion and why Jeremy now has your job."

Manny turned pleading eyes to Debbie, but her face was set resolutely, and she just shook her head.

Manny stood up, fury glittering from his dark eyes. "You'll rue this day, you bitches," he hissed. "You're both dykes." He lumbered to the door and slammed it behind him.

Amanda's voice buzzed into Debbie's phone. "Debbie, I've called security. Manny headed to his office. I've already voided his access to our computer system, but—"

"Just keep an eye on his door until security arrives," Debbie told her. "They shouldn't be more than a few minutes. Tell them to make sure that Manny leaves immediately after he cleans out his desk. I do not want him admitted to the building again for any reason." She sat down heavily in her chair, and sighed.

"It's too much every day," Sheila quipped tiredly. "He's the third one I've had to fire. I hope you don't regret making me VP."

Debbie shook her head. "You're finding out Pandora's weaknesses, Sheila. While Paul was part of this company, a lot of his friends with less than savory reputations got hired. I'd probably have gotten rid of them eventually anyway just because I didn't feel I could trust them. But when you've got concrete proof that they were and have been sandbagging us,

I'm not going to hesitate to act."

"One of the things I just adore about you," Sheila said with a smile, then looked away quickly.

Debbie stared at her. *It had never crossed her mind that Sheila could be her secret admirer because she was a woman. But there had been more than sociable affection in her friend's tone.*

"I do have good news," Sheila said without looking up. "Giorgio found a way through that red tape problem. We can leave all the seduction scenes in *Hell's Gate* uncut without losing even one of our bookings for the film."

"Ah!" Debbie laughed with relief and excitement. "Wonderful! But are you sure even the scene with the demon and the virgin is—"

"The official film rating is still PG-13," Sheila said confidently. "I sat with the ratings guy myself through his screening of it. While he was clearly uncomfortable with the footage, he said that the seduction is clearly not rape by the dialogue and actions of the couple, so it's not an R-rated scene." She smiled. "Don't you just love these grey areas?"

"What I think is that our new edginess as a production company is going to give me an ulcer," Debbie retorted. She raised her hand quickly, as Sheila stared at her, her friend's shock clearly turning to irritation. "But you're right that we needed to push the envelope, Sheila. The public wants it, and even the mainstream movies are showing total male nudity in some R films. We need to not only keep up with that line in the sand; we need to nudge it in the ass a little in an artistic way. You've done that perfectly, Sheila."

Sheila sighed. "I worry sometimes you don't like what I've done with your company."

"If I hadn't, I wouldn't have promoted you," Debbie said affectionately. Sheila looked up happily. Debbie flushed. Again in Sheila's eyes was not only friendship, but something more.

"It's close to five," Debbie said, throwing a stack of papers across the desk. "Go home. As Scarlett said, 'Tomorrow is another day'."

"Are you going home?" Sheila asked, even as she got up from her chair.

"Yes," Debbie lied. "Get going. We've got that early meeting at eight with that promotional company. We've got to be sharp as knives."

"Then you'd better practice your acting," Sheila teased with a smile. "Your level is only about Vivian's now." Before Debbie could answer, Sheila ducked out of the office.

Debbie leaned back in her chair, Sheila's mention of Vivian and the girl's lies leading her thoughts back to the Black Rose and her secret admirer. Another three weeks had gone by, and she was no closer to finding out who'd given her the gift. She'd have to lean on Vivian's boss at her upcoming appointment next week.

But what to do about Sheila? While Debbie didn't want a relationship with her beyond friendship, she didn't want to hurt Sheila, either. Sheila had become invaluable to Pandora in the short time she'd been here.

An easy solution would be to find Sheila someone else…but then she risked Sheila being corrupted by an asshole the way Rebecca had been. If only there was an easy solution. Maybe she should try being bi herself?

Debbie laughed aloud, then got her coat and hat. She was probably being stupid, and had thought she'd seen something where there was nothing.

As she walked to her car, Debbie faced that she did have one overdue action item on her calendar that was growing more urgent and would have to be faced: her lack of a boyfriend. While there were men she could approach to hook up with, Debbie wanted more than a few hours of sex once a week. The problem was she had no prospects. The thought was sobering, and occupied Debbie's thoughts all the way home.

Being with Paul had subdued something in her during those months of their farce affair, but it was finally reawakening. She hadn't liked who she was when she was with him, and sex had become something she faked as fast as she could. But these past months, she had begun noticing men again: the way they moved, their deep voices, the way they often towered over her female frame. Debbie had to be the one in control from dawn to dusk. She wanted someone else to take care of her from dusk to dawn.

She smiled as she drove into her garage, then turned on her lights. It was so much more homey, having a house instead of her apartment. Like everything else in that first month, the house had been easy to find, the perfect location and so affordable Debbie had had to ask twice to make sure that the price the agent quoted was real.

The house wasn't a coincidence however. That had been Shaker's doing. Debbie thought back to that fateful evening, savoring the events.

Shaker had come home—*arrived in her apartment,* she corrected quickly—and handed her an address and a name of a realtor. "Call about it in a week," the demon had said. "Affordable and private. Perfect for you in other words, Mistress."

Debbie had smiled as she took the paper. "What did you do, kill the current owners?"

Shaker had laughed, the deep sound like the earth cracking open. "You're so refreshing for a human, Mistress. Yes, of course I did." He kissed her hand, his hot lips reddening her skin. "Murder always lowers property values. But don't worry. They'll replace the carpets before they put it up for sale."

Debbie had been horrified. She'd nodded dumbly, then sat down on the nearest chair.

Shaker had come over at once, going to one knee before her as he folded up his hooved leg beneath him. "I see I've disturbed you. Why? I've no wish to hurt you, so you shouldn't fear me. But it shouldn't be a surprise that I'm going to kill other humans from time to time. I eat human flesh, Mistress."

Debbie had clutched the chair arms tightly, dizzy. "You ate them?"

"The demon diet is a narrow one," Shaker admitted. "Believe me, I'd sooner be eating chocolate and hamburgers. They don't require dismemberment."

Debbie laughed, the edges of the noise so brittle her hysteria went up a notch.

"But enough of this nasty subject," Shaker said soothingly. "You've had another long day. Want me to draw you a bath? Or perhaps a back massage?"

Debbie had let him draw her bath, then told Shaker she wanted to be alone. But the bath hadn't soothed her at all…

Debbie pushed the thought away, surveying her new house. Shaker had been right in one aspect: the house was gorgeous and perfect for her. While the commute took a good 45 minutes, having a yard of her own and two bedrooms was worth it. Best of all, the woods at the back of the house were state land. Every morning there were deer munching grass and rabbits frolicking on the lawn. It was nice to watch them in the mornings and relax a bit before heading into Pandora and its never-ending problems…

"Mistress?" Shaker said, appearing beside her. "Do you want anything tonight, or would you prefer to be left alone?"

Debbie looked at him uneasily. Since his confession of murder, she had asked him most nights to leave her. At first, she'd been worried her commands would anger him, but Shaker just nodded each evening and disappeared.

There had been enough of intrigue. Debbie had too many unanswered questions. It was time she faced up to the truth. "I need answers to some questions, Shaker. And I need the truth."

Shaker inclined his head amicably. "You have only to ask."

"Did you do something to help with Dante?"

Shaker nodded. "He's a slippery one, otherwise he'd have already met with a nasty accident like his dad. But I found it far easier to distract than destroy." He leaned back against the doorway frame, making it creak in protest. "You'd be surprised how easy that is."

"What did you do? Exact actions, Shaker."

"Apologies, Mistress. I was not aware you wanted particulars. I appeared in front of his lover's car on the road. She crashed it—predictably—and broke several bones. His father's promotional company, Panko Promos, was in bankruptcy, as you know. That was not my doing, but I also arranged for the CEO to think he needed to flee to Mexico." Shaker smiled. "Not hard to do, since it was his actions that had led to the financial woes. But I helped him decide to destroy all his files. With no backup, Paul is not going to be able to rally from that bankruptcy. Point of fact, that meeting you have tomorrow is not about promos for Pandora, but is an emissary from Dante asking for you to buy his company in an effort to save it—and his stock—from annihilation."

Debbie stared at Shaker. "Panko isn't coming to meet with me. The name is—"

"Paul tried renaming the company in an effort to avoid his creditors, but that failed," Shaker interrupted. "I think you'll find the company an asset, with the right person at the helm. And you can give it a new name. One with a bit more flair, perhaps?"

"That's good," Debbie said, feeling relieved at no mention of blood or dismemberment. "What else did you do? Pandora has had a run of good luck recently."

"I've been busy of late," Shaker intoned seriously, then laughed. "Mostly a few words in the right people's ears. As you know I can appear and disappear anywhere practically at will. You have a good quality company, Mistress. Just a few notes left on a desk or whispered reminders during sleep are enough to get some good people interested in working with you, such as that actor Jett Black."

"And the governmental red tape? I heard it's no longer an issue."

"The red tape I can't take credit for. Giorgio did that on his own, with a few sexual favors. But as both parties enjoyed themselves from what I saw, I'm not sure it's even immoral."

"Did you instigate that?" Debbie asked.

"I don't need to encourage lust in humans as a rule," Shaker replied easily. "Your race manages that in spades on its own with no assistance from the demon world."

"What about the new pictures Sheila procured? Or our new set artist Caroline, whose scenery is unbelievably real yet seems to cost us almost nothing? Or Saul—?"

"You know, you really surprise me, Mistress. Wanting to know the gory details is usually strictly a male request—"

"Tell me the Goddamn truth, Shaker!" Debbie shouted angrily. "Did you have a hand in this?"

Shaker strode toward Debbie, his red eyes glowing in the dimness of the room. An evil feeling snaked its way through the room, making Debbie shiver.

"You know I did. I made sure there were no offers on those pictures. All but one buyer was persuaded solely with the evil feeling of my presence whenever they acted to procure the film rights...that same evil that is making you tremble now. Then I drove the one buyer who wouldn't back down insane with images of torture every time he went to sleep.

"Caroline is an acquaintance who was looking for work. All you need to know is she has magical ability, which is where all those cost savings come from. She knows how to keep her head down and produce, and that is all you need to know."

Debbie opened her mouth to speak, but Shaker took another step closer, silencing her.

"Hiring Saul was Manny's doing, not mine. I killed him tonight, framing Manny for the deed easily." Shaker laughed. "Manny will likely kill himself with a little prodding. Smile, Mistress. Your flop of a picture just got a hell of a lot more exclusive with a dead lead."

Debbie sat down hard in her easy chair, her mind reeling. "Actors die every day of overdose or accidents on the set, Shaker. It's not a big—"

"Not one who was stabbed twenty-seven times in their billiard room with the broken end of a pool cue," Shaker stated with a grin. "Not one active in seven separate charities with a loving trophy wife who was captured on film holding the ragged remains of her husband by her astute stepchild. He'll be selling those pictures before dawn comes for a pile of money." Shaker laughed. "The wife herself will likely contact you about donating all Saul's proceeds from the film. In any case, Pandora will benefit immensely."

"I never asked you to kill anyone," Debbie said defensively. "I never asked you to—"

"You asked me to save your company, and I've done it," Shaker shouted, the boom of his voice shaking the room like a small earthquake. He loomed over her. "What did you think was going to happen? I'm a demon out of Hell! What did you think I would do when you unleashed me on your enemies?"

"These are human beings—"

"Who matter as much as insects splattered on a windshield," Shaker snarled. "Humans are just another species who think that they are superior to all others…a prevalent notion in all evolved creatures. They are not." He stared down at her. "You are not superior to me, Mistress."

Debbie looked up at him with tear-filled eyes. "But I am human. How do I know you won't hurt me, too, Shaker?"

"Honestly?" he said gruffly, his expression softening. "You don't. But the same could be said of any human man you know, Mistress." He leaned in closer, tilting his head. "And I kiss better than most."

Debbie didn't know what to do when the demon's lips met hers. She leaned back involuntarily, but Shaker just leaned forward farther, his lips pressing hers. His kiss was nothing like she'd expected it to be: not brutally strong, or too hot, or even too provocative. It began as a chaste kiss; gentle, languid, warm, with just a hint of passion to come if the merest sign was given. The longer it went on, the hotter Debbie got, the urge to open her mouth growing each moment. Just as she gave in and relaxed into Shaker's embrace, he pulled back from her, ending the kiss, his red eyes staring into hers, his desire mirroring her desire.

"Part of the contract we have, Debbie Deal, is for me to guard you. In the event you should die, I go to Hell. I am only out of Hell now because of your acquiescence to my proposal on our partnership."

"How did you get out to proposition me in the first place, then?" Debbie asked, trying to collect her wits.

"I'm allowed out to do that, in a given set time frame," Shaker replied. "If you hadn't agreed, I'd have been recalled back to Hell."

"Is Hell real?"

"Lake of Fire, the Gates, endless tortures, etc...yes, it's all real," Shaker said with a laugh. "But hardly as described. Most humans think they did terrible things. But in the scheme of the universe, there is a pretty big sliding scale on what is truly evil."

"Tell me everything," Debbie asked, enrapt.

Shaker laughed again, but there was something sad about this particular laugh. It made Debbie wonder how much of Shaker's easy attitude was real, and how much covered a deep sorrow. "Wouldn't you rather talk about something else, human, besides death?"

"Why don't you want to tell me?" Debbie pressed, pushing the hand that had been reaching out for him back into her lap.

"Because you're bound to me," Shaker said softly, caressing her cheek with his taloned hand. "And that means your fate after you die is sealed, Mistress. You will never enter the gates of Heaven unless you give me up." He leaned in close again. "And I don't intend to let you go."

The kiss this time was powerful, primal, seductive, and hotter than hell. Debbie succumbed at once, throwing her arms around Shaker and embracing him, her mouth opening on his. Shaker had deepened the kiss, his tongue probing and tangling with Debbie's, tasting her. In a minute, her yearning for him was unbearable.

Debbie closed her eyes, her thoughts turning back to that day, and gave a soft moan, her face flushing in remembered wantonness.

Shaker had stood with Debbie in his arms, and carried her into her bedroom. Setting her gently on the bed, Shaker had lain down beside her, then began to take off her clothes.

"I can get those," Debbie had said impatiently, pushing his hands away. "Take off yours."

"I have little to remove," Shaker replied, his deep voice rumbling with lust. Yet he began untying the loincloth he had always worn in her presence.

Debbie stripped off her clothes then turned to Shaker. Her mouth dropped open at the sheer size of him. What she had assumed would be comparable to a couple of tomatoes approached grapefruit size…

"Yes, we demons are well-hung, so to speak," Shaker chuckled. "But I assure you I'll be gentle, Mistress. Would you like to be on top?"

"No," Debbie stammered quickly. "You."

Shaker moved atop her. Instead of a quick copulation, his seduction of her continued, his kisses passionate as his hands roamed her body. Carefully, gently, he entered, then began thrusting.

Debbie stopped him. "Wait."

"Yes?" Shaker intoned.

"I…um, we…should there be protection?"

"I can easily arrange a fruitless coupling," Shaker said with a chuckle as he resumed motion. "Lay back and enjoy, Mistress. I am planning more than several lengthy acts, so you must conserve your strength." He kissed down her throat, eliciting an eager moan from Debbie. "Your pleasure is paramount in our play."

* * * *

Afterwards, Debbie lay sated in Shaker's arms, still trying to comprehend what she had done.

"Yes, Mistress," Shaker whispered, kissing her cheek. "You have bedded a demon. Several times, in point."

"Are you sure you're…that we're safe?" Debbie said urgently. With her reason returned, the ramifications of what she'd done were spinning through her head.

"It's rare that a human beds a demon looking for a half-demon child," Shaker said, in between kisses. "I'm a being for orgy sex, not easy Sunday mornings doing the crossword in bed over coffee. And it's easy enough to accomplish."

"How?"

"Do you really want to know particulars?" Shaker asked in a cool tone. "Last time—"

"No," Debbie said quickly. "I just can count the number of times I had unprotected sex on one hand, and that was all in high school with the same kid. And you're…supernatural."

"If you are so rational as to be hung up on such base details, I can see I'll have to perform better next time," Shaker teased. "Provided there is a next time, of course."

Debbie lay silent, not sure how to reply. What did he expect her to say? The sex had been great, yes. But it had just been sex for both of them.

Shaker gently distanced himself, standing and retying his loincloth. "It's very late, Mistress. I'll leave you to sleep."

"Thank you," Debbie said awkwardly, pulling up the sheet to cover her naked body.

"I also must bring up the subject of favors," Shaker mentioned, turning back to Debbie. "I've expended a great deal of energy on your behalf. It's time for you to hold up your end of our deal."

Debbie stared at Shaker, her post coital bliss fading away. "What do you need?"

"Sustenance," Shaker said with a toothy grin.

"Souls?"

"Something like that," Shaker said. "But it's more of a collaborative effort than an exchange of goods."

"Can we do it the first week of March?" Debbie said, her mind racing. "This next week is booked solid."

"Of course," Shaker said with a nod. "Goodnight."

Chapter Three

~ February ~

What had happened? Debbie sat at her desk, wondering how so much had gone wrong so fast.

February had ended beautifully. Shaker's information about Dante's financial straits and his offer to buy his promotional company had been correct. Debbie had agreed, after a little negotiating. Panko Promotions had already become Pandora Promotions, a new division of her company. Dante had been paid a pittance for a business easily worth ten times the price Debbie had paid, and had been grateful for it.

Tinderbox had re-released to the highest first weekend gross ever for Pandora. Saul's death had been a huge publicity boon to the film, and his widow had even gone on a tour to promote the film with her own funds, saying that her husband's last work needed to be memorialized. Critics were saying the film was a "triumph," an "epic showing Saul's unrecognized genius as an actor." Manny had committed suicide as Shaker had prophesied, the bloody murder weapon found beneath his bed tying up all loose ends. Pandora seemed poised to become queen of the independent film studios.

Then had come the first of March.

Debbie had arrived in the office to a panicked Giorgio practically wringing his hands in distress. "The ratings guy who approved the seduction scenes in *Hell's Gate* quit his job. His replacement reviewed the film and said that it was a clear cut R-rating. He won't budge."

Debbie had sent Giorgio back to plead with the head of the ratings board. Sheila had come running in as soon as he'd gone, her expression murderous. "Did Giorgio tell you about the ratings guy?"

Debbie nodded. "We're too far in to do anything but eat the cost if the film release in anything higher than PG-13. We need that young teen audience, or we won't even break even. We'll have to delay it."

"At least we won't have such a big cost outlay on our next films," Sheila assured. "Caroline has to be a witch; she's so good stretching pennies into full backdrops."

Probably true, Debbie thought darkly. "Are we still on for meeting with Titan's reps at noon?"

Sheila nodded. "All prepped. But we do have another problem."

"Which is?"

"Jett Black was in an accident—"

"What happened?" Debbie demanded. "Can he still work? All our cash is tied up in *Smoke and Ashes*. That has to be on schedule to release for this Christmas."

"It shouldn't be a problem," Sheila assured. "His leg is broken in three places, but production thinks they can work around it with stunt doubles. They'd already shot a lot of the action scenes, and most of what was left was dialogue and close ups."

Debbie sat down heavily in her office chair. "What happened to him?"

"Skiing accident," Sheila said glumly. "Didn't I tell you that our luck was bound to run out sooner or later?"

Debbie closed her eyes, her thoughts frantic. *She hadn't given Shaker his favor. By putting it off, had she brought this bad luck down on Pandora?*

"I do have good news," Sheila said. "We've put most everything into *Smoke and Ashes*, like I've said. But I was able to secure rights to *Absolution* last week. We'll need only five actors total, and most of the emphasis is on the main couple, so if we shot in some Midwestern town and saved most of the budget for the lead, we'll—"

"Do me a favor," Debbie said heavily. "Go check right now that the deal is solid and that there are no gaps or wiggle room. Okay?"

Sheila looked at her oddly. "I'll check, but I'm 99% sure."

"It's that last percentage I'm worried about," Debbie replied. "Please check again anyway. When it rains it pours."

Later that afternoon, Debbie and Sheila smiled falsely as three Titan reps sat down across from them in the main Pandora conference room. Then Dante entered, eyes glittering with malice.

Debbie wanted to snarl, but she made herself smile. "Dante, how nice to see you. So you're working for Titan now?"

"Sure," Dante answered, taking a seat. "Dad sent me to film school, as I'm sure you know. It was always in the cards that I would come to work at Pandora someday."

In your wet dreams. "I'm not sure I understand," Debbie said politely.

"Then let me explain," one of the Titan reps said. "I'm sure you are aware that Titan wanted to procure Pandora, but you'd refused to honor the proposed deal, as was your right. And we certainly can't tell the president of a company what to do."

"But your shareholders can," Dante added vengefully.

"We don't have shareholders," Debbie said pointedly. "Paul had proposed it numerous times, but Becky always vetoed him along with me."

"Until last December," the Titan rep said, handing both Debbie and Sheila a thickly stapled packet. "Rebecca Pall signed along with her husband to take the company public. They planned to release ten thousand shares initially. Three thousand belong to you—"

"And three thousand belonged to Paul and Rebecca," Dante said triumphantly. "I have six thousand shares to your three, Debbie."

"—with the remaining thousand slated to be released to the public for sale, all proceeds to benefit Pandora," the Titan rep finished, with a look of reproach for Dante. "This sale was supposed to take place in January of this year, but with the matter of Paul Pall's disappearance, it was delayed."

"Was Paul's body found?" Debbie inquired, knowing it could not have been.

"No," Dante said. "But I know my father. He would never have gone off and left without a word to me. So I petitioned to have him legally declared dead." He handed Debbie a piece of paper. "It was signed this morning."

Debbie's mind raced. "What exactly is your proposition?"

"That I take over Pandora for Titan Pictures," Dante said. "You can either work with us, or against us. But one way or another, you'll be out by the end of this year."

"You sniveling shit," Sheila whispered.

"Ms. Deal," the Titan rep said. "I believe I should speak to you alone. Can that be arranged?"

Dante whipped his head around and stared. "That wasn't mentioned to me."

"And I'm not here on your dollar, but on Titan's," the man said sharply. He turned to his two coworkers. "Please take Mr. Pall outside, if he can't find the door by himself."

They rose without a word and Dante went with them, muttering angrily. Sheila also left, with one uneasy look back at Debbie.

When they were alone, the Titan rep extended his hand. "Let's begin again," he said with a conspiratorial wink. "My name is Henry Castle."

Debbie shook his hand reluctantly. "And you know mine, Mr. Castle. So please say what you came to say."

"Off the record," Henry said, leaning back in his chair. "Titan has kept track of the changes you've made at Pandora. While admittedly more risky than what we would have done, you've certainly become a force to be reckoned with in the film industry. Even the death of one of your leading men seems to have become a boon for you."

You've no idea, Debbie thought. "We've had a run of good luck, which sadly seems to have ended very disastrously."

"Maybe not," Henry said seriously. "This is not the done deal that Dante has professed it to be."

Debbie's eyes narrowed. "What do you mean?"

"I mean that having someone declared dead with no real proof is risky. As you are likely aware, there was no body, and no sign of foul play other than some knocked over office furniture. Your statement to the police—and Rebecca's, I might add—say that Paul left the office last New Year's Eve alive. If Paul is discovered to be alive, Dante will be barred from inheriting the shares through his father's will."

"Why are you helping me?" Debbie asked point blank.

Henry ignored her question. "Additionally, Dante's date of his death for his father predeceases his stepmother's. His father's will—wisely, but in blatant discordance to the doting dad that his son paints him as—left everything to Rebecca with a stipulated amount for his son. Rebecca's will, however, is another story. She was far more thorough about her wishes being carried out and updated her will regularly. She left her shares of Pandora equally to you and Paul, with the bulk of her money going to charity and the rest to Paul. So when the dust settles, you and Dante will have the same amount of stock."

Must have been before she found out about Paul and me, and decided to kill me. God Becky, I hope you're in a better place. "And the remaining stock?"

"Shareholders who control the majority of a company's shares effectively have enough voting power to dictate the firm's decisions," Henry said. "If you can obtain the other shares, you'll retain power over Pandora." He handed her a paper. "Making the stock available to the public is something I have agreed to handle for Dante, who is executor of Rebecca's will as Rebecca's nearest living kin. Titan wants Pandora more than ever."

"Then why are you telling me?" Debbie said bitterly. "This is a done deal, Henry."

"The sale of the remaining shares of Pandora stock will not take place until end of December," Henry placated, his hand upraised. "You have time, just not a lot. Make use of it, Debbie."

Debbie slammed her palm down hard on the table, making Henry jump and her hand sting. "Why are you helping me?"

"Because I don't trust that weasel kid any more than you do," Henry replied. "I suspect that Paul is alive, though I don't understand why he's missing. In any case, Titan's official position—on my advice—is to wait and see what you do with Pandora. You may double the company's worth by the end of the year. The price for the stock was already decided on, so any increase in value is sheer profit for us. Titan buying all the stock for sale will not be an issue, with me arranging the sale. The only benefit to pushing through the stock sale right now is to Dante, who thinks because he's agreed to sell us all his shares that he's somehow going to be made boss." Henry laughed. "That's not going to happen."

"Why tell me all this?" Debbie said, relief at being given more time palpable in her tone. "You've given me information you could have easily kept to yourself."

"Because I liked your pictures through the years," Henry said kindly, packing up his papers. "*Tinderbox* wasn't the gem it was made out to be, but I've read the script to *Smoke and Ashes*. It is very good, and definitely a movie worth making." He closed his briefcase and stood. "If you had one huge hit on a mainstream level, Debbie, Titan would likely give you free rein with Pandora, as well as honor the deal Rebecca had worked out for you." His expression softened. "Why don't you take the afternoon off to think about it? This has to come as a shock. Get a massage or something."

Debbie stared at Henry. *This was him. It had to be. Here was her secret admirer.* She stood up, then extended her hand. "I may do that. Thank you for the information, Henry."

"You're welcome," he said in the same soft tone.

"Are you fond of roses?" Debbie said casually, watching Henry carefully. "You know they come in all colors, even black."

Henry looked back at her quizzically. "Yes, I like them. Do you, Debbie?"

"Yes," Debbie said, giving him a rare genuine smile. "I do."

Henry gave her a smile, then left, shutting the door behind him.

Debbie put her head down on her arms, all her tension leaving her limp as a rag doll. *No wonder she hadn't guessed. How could she have guessed that a man who worked for Titan would be on her side? But was his gift a simple gesture of kindness, or was this all an elaborate effort to manipulate her?*

Sheila banged in the door, her expression steamed. "What did he say? Did he make you cry? What happened?"

"He's...he was helpful," Debbie said, then filled in her friend on what Henry had said.

"So he's the one?" Sheila said thoughtfully. "I wouldn't have guessed either. He's nice enough looking anyway."

Debbie didn't answer, lost in thought.

"I'm afraid I do have more bad news," Sheila said slowly. "Remember how I said I could save money on setting by filming *Absolution* in a small town? Well, the town we booked is flooded. They got ten inches of rain in eight hours. They agreed to negate the contract, but they kept the deposit—"

Debbie let out a breath. "Is it close to noon?"

Sheila glanced at her watch. "Five minutes to."

Debbie stood up, stretching. "Get your coat. We're taking the rest of the day off."

Sheila looked at her, bewildered. "But we've got a host of problems, Deb. I actually thought you'd want to postpone today's scheduled visit to The Black Rose."

"No," Debbie said resolutely. "I need it, Sheila. Come on. The problems will still be here tomorrow."

* * * *

As soon as Debbie arrived home that night, she called Shaker's name. He appeared before her at once.

"Sex," Debbie said, beginning to strip off her clothes. "Now, please."

Shaker grinned, and began untying his loincloth. "As you wish, Mistress."

* * * *

Debbie lay in her Jacuzzi, Shaker opposite her, his legs entwined with hers.

"Careful with those hooves," Debbie said, wincing. "They're sharper than they look."

Shaker reached out for her and pulled her onto his lap with a splash. "Sit here, Mistress. Then you'll not have to deal with those base parts of me."

"I will have to deal with another base part, however," Debbie teased, stroking his skin with her hands. Shaker smiled and leaned back, putting his arms behind his head.

"What is your favor?" Debbie said, after a moment of silence.

Shaker smiled. "Like I said, sustenance."

44

"Elaborate in specific terms."

"All right," Shaker replied. "In specific terms, I need to eat. I've killed for you several times now, but usually I've had to leave the body as evidence for the police. I'm very hungry, Mistress. In simple terms, you need to provide for me."

"You're saying I need to kill someone?"

"Not necessarily," Shaker replied. "But you do need to choose whom I consume. And I do have to warn you that everybody is not available for the choosing."

"Like who?"

"Like priests," Shaker said, steadying Debbie as she shifted on his lap to face him fully. "I have a hard time consuming anyone of faith. Faith is a demon's enemy."

"Like a cross?"

Shaker brushed that aside. "A cross without faith is two lines. Any symbol without faith is only a talisman. But true faith in any form is toxic, talisman or no."

Debbie looked at Shaker worriedly. "You mean you can die?"

"I can be destroyed here in the flesh," Shaker amended, scooping some water to run over Debbie's bare back. "But my essence will always survive. I can always live again."

"So you can come back to me? That's a kind of immortality—"

Shaker stopped still. "If something happens to me, Mistress, the shock of it will hurt you, also. It may also possibly kill you, if I sustain a mortal wound."

Debbie looked down at him, irate. "Why are you only mentioning these important points when I drag them out of you?"

"Don't be bitchy," Shaker said pleasantly, scooping up more water to bathe Debbie. "I'm bound by Hell's laws to cause as much fear and suffering as possible in this world. That goes in tandem with my rules that I have to follow for humans bound to me. I have to transverse a complex web, Mistress."

Debbie grabbed Shaker's hand, stopping him. "Which means?"

Shaker gave her a dour look. "Which means I don't like Hell. I don't like being there when I could be here in a Jacuzzi with someone like you,

Mistress. I'm happy to smooth over the nasty bits of our arrangement to make it as pleasant as possible for you."

"Essentially, you just justified keeping me in the dark," Debbie accused, moving to get out.

Shaker grabbed hold of her, his taloned hands keeping her from leaving. "If you hadn't taken my offer, you'd be dead by Rebecca's curse, and Paul would have arranged a quick demise for her and be enjoying hookers in the Caribbean. Without you at the helm, Pandora would have gone down in flames. Even if by some miracle you had lived, you'd have lost your job and be working now as a lackey at some two-bit film company, still living in your crappy apartment—if you could even afford it! So stop with the second-guessing! You would not have acted differently back then knowing what you know now."

He was right, damn him. "What else are you not telling me?" Debbie said in a small voice.

Shaker caressed her cheek, then kissed her. "You have more than enough on your plate, Debbie. Don't ask for more right now." He kissed her again. "We are partners in this, after a fashion. Trust me that I'll make you aware of anything that affects our partnership and you in any way."

"The favor you need affects me," Debbie retorted, pushing him away. "No more games. What do you need me to do?"

"Pick someone. It can be anyone; I'll tell you if they aren't suitable. Ideally, you'd choose someone that already has some black mark on their soul from doing evil."

"Like being bound to a demon?" Debbie said sarcastically.

"No," Shaker said seriously. "Believe me, you do not want to send any demon to Hell purposefully by killing their human counterpart. As soon as they get out again—and they always do—the first order of business after they bind with a new human is to seek out the person who sent them to Hell last time. They'll come back again and again until they've killed their enemy." He kissed her. "But you don't have to worry about that. I'll check out that aspect on any people you choose to make sure they aren't bound."

Shaker was logical, she had to give him that. And more than a passing strategist. "Are all demons so reasonable?" Debbie teased.

"The old ones like me are," Shaker rumbled lustily, moving Debbie so she sat astride him. "Who wants to be always looking over their shoulder? There are much more pleasurable things to do." He let out a groan as their lips touched, then Shaker forcefully deepened the kiss.

Debbie's desire was rising again, but she pushed it down, moving back from Shaker. "So I can choose anyone? Even a random stranger?"

Shaker nodded. "But try to choose someone who won't be missed. Someone with a huge family is not a good idea. Think loners, homeless people, criminals, orphans, or kids with parents who don't care. They are all good prospects." He kissed her again. "A degree of distance is also a good idea, at least for the majority. If everyone you know begins to go missing, officials such as police tend to take an interest, as a rule."

How could he be so cold about it? "What if I gave you the choice?" Debbie said, pushing him away again. "So long as it was no one I knew?"

"That is allowed," Shaker said thoughtfully. "But I'd advise you to think twice, Mistress. It's a small world sometimes. People's lives are often more interrelated than you suspect."

Debbie wasn't sure what he meant, but she didn't care. The lust that had been building in her wasn't going to be denied. "Sit on the edge of the tub," she commanded. "I want you."

Shaker obeyed, his rumble of pleasure loud as Debbie straddled him and began moving.

* * * *

The next morning, Debbie walked into her office refreshed and ready to deal with Pandora's recent difficulties. What she was not ready for was the two dozen roses on her desk, their rainbow of colors vibrant.

"They came this morning," Amanda said, sticking her head in the doorway. She came over to Debbie, handing her a small card in an open envelope.

Debbie opened it, but before she could read it, Amanda said gleefully, "And who is Henry? Come on, I want all the details!"

Debbie flushed, then took out the card.

I hope some of these are your favorite color. Would you like to have dinner this week?
-Henry

Debbie put the card back in its envelope. "Amanda, did you read this?"

"The envelope was open," Amanda said defensively. "There was no name on the card. I thought they might have been for me."

A logical explanation...and maybe the truth. But what else would Amanda poke her nose into next? Maybe something that Debbie would regret. "It's okay. You're right—there is no name on the card."

"I'll be at my desk if you need me," Amanda said icily, obviously miffed. She stalked out.

Debbie called the flower delivery company, then explained who she was. "Tell me, did the person who delivered my flowers know they were for me?"

There was a pause. "Yes, Ms. Deal. Our paperwork says that your secretary signed for you, as you weren't there."

Amanda had known the flowers weren't for her. She also was in a position to make things hard for Henry if she discovered that he had been the one that sent the flowers. Titan would not look kindly on an employee giving a company that was being taken over inside information.

She needed Henry, at least until she figured out if he was sincere or a plant. And either way, she needed him in position at Titan.

Amada would have to go. She'd tell Shaker tonight.

* * * *

"You're sure on this?" Shaker said again. "Your secretary is the one?"

"Her name is Amanda," Debbie said crossly. "And yes, I'm sure. She's always been about the paycheck and nothing else. But now her nosiness is growing. I need her removed before she says anything to Titan about Henry."

48

A Good Year

"I doubt that she would have the brains to do so, from what I've seen of her," Shaker said, after a moment. "But your will is my path." He disappeared.

Debbie smiled to herself, then realization flooded her, making her heart race. She had never mentioned Henry by name. *Why hadn't Shaker asked who Henry was? She hadn't mentioned the flowers or anything about her admirer to Shaker. How did he already know?*

Chapter Four

~ March ~

Debbie wasn't sure what to expect the next morning. She worried irrationally that she'd come into the office and Shaker would be sitting in Amanda's chair, grinning at her with a bloody smile. But instead the office was locked tight, as it should have been.

Debbie unlocked the door, and went inside. Amanda's things were on her desk, her small potted plant slightly wilted. Near it was a small picture frame of a little girl in a white communion dress.

Celia. Debbie picked up the frame, letting out a sigh. Amanda had stopped mentioning the little girl two years before. She had been killed in an auto accident by a drunk driver over four years ago. Since then, Amada had pretty much kept to herself. She'd been on her way to spinsterhood, her husband also dead of a heart attack a full six years before.

It was almost a blessing to speed her on her way to join them…

Horrified at her thoughts, Amanda put the picture down quickly, then bustled to her office. She picked up the phone, and called Human Resources, reporting Amanda's absence, and asking them to call her house. "I know it's still early, but she's never late. Give a call, just in case she overslept, please."

The rest of the morning was frantic, filled with all the normal Monday crises. Debbie quickly forgot about Amanda. At five o'clock, Sheila came trudging in, her step tired but her face elated.

"Remember the setting problem? I solved it. We can shoot the next town over. They have a place with the same mountain as a backdrop. It'll be perfect." Sheila plopped down into the chair. "So your secretary never showed up?"

Guilt flooded Debbie. *I did it. I had her killed. God, is it always so hard? Maybe it's better to give Shaker full choice over his victims...*

"Are you listening to me?" Sheila said sharply. "Earth to Debbie. Come in, please."

"Sorry," Debbie said with a fake yawn. "I'm just tired. I didn't get much sleep last night."

Sheila stood, her expression understanding. "Then you should head home. I'm giving up for today myself. Do you want to walk down to the garage?"

Debbie nodded, grabbing her jacket. "Let's go."

* * * *

Shaker stayed away for the next week. Debbie was anxious, wondering if something had happened to him. But he appeared that Saturday night as she lounged in the tub, reading some erotica. This time, like never before, he was naked.

"I see I chose the right moment to arrive," Shaker said, taking her book from her hands. "And what new things have you learned from this reading research, my Mistress?"

"Come here and see," Debbie said, beckoning with a sexy smile.

* * * *

Afterwards, neither mentioned Amanda, or anything to do with favors. But Debbie was conscious of Shaker's heat and his desire, both of which seemed much more powerful than they had ever been before.

"Mistress," Shaker said as they laid in her bed entwined. "I was wondering if you'd like to accompany me to a festival of sorts."

Debbie did a double take. "Are you asking me on a date?"

Shaker laughed. "More of a party. But technically, yes, I suppose you could call it a date."

"And where do demons go to party?" Debbie quipped.

"There is a pagan holiday called Beltane celebrated on Mayday, which is May first. Usually a few weeks before that holiday there is a gathering of demons that celebrate a parody of it."

"Is it safe?"

"As safe as general debauchery usually is," Shaker replied. "We don't have to stay long. But I do have a few friends who I'd like to see. As you stipulated in your right-to-know speech a few weeks ago, these beings would be good for you to be aware of. And it would also be good for you if they were aware of you."

Debbie was not sure she wanted other demons to be aware of her. Yet Shaker likely wouldn't have recommended it if there was any danger to her. "Will there be other humans there like me? Those that have demons?"

Shaker nodded. "Yes. Be prepared that you'll see all manner of things. But there is no requirement to participate in any of the events or festivities. The basic tenet of demon reveling is do what pleases you."

"I'll go if you'll take me home when I want to leave," Debbie said, nodding.

"Thank you," Shaker said, something like gratefulness in his tone. Before Debbie could reply, he pushed her back gently on her back. "Now let me show you the depth of my appreciation for you, Mistress."

* * * *

"Where are you?" Sheila demanded, her irate tone snapping Debbie out of her fog. "You haven't heard a word I've said. What is on your mind, Debbie? Nothing should be, besides how we're going to get the funding for *Absolution*! *Smoke and Ashes* is already over budget and it's only half done!"

"I'm sorry," Debbie said weakly. "I just—"

"What has you so distracted?" Sheila shouted. "Answer me and tell the truth this time!"

"Demon sex," Debbie said tiredly, then clapped her hand over her mouth.

Sheila gaped at her.

"I'm sorry," Debbie said quickly, flushing. "I haven't been sleeping, and—"

"You said demon sex," Sheila said flatly. "Don't bullshit me. Which demon have you been sleeping with? It wouldn't be our newly healed star, Jett Black, would it?"

There was copious jealousy in Sheila's tone. Worse, she had taken Debbie's admission to mean an actor playing a demon in film, not a real demon. She'd never believe that Debbie wasn't fucking one of the leading men.

"I've not seen Jett since—"

"Then who is it?" Sheila yelled. "Who have you been fucking?"

"Why do you care?" Debbie yelled right back. "Who I fuck is my business, not yours!"

Sheila glared at Debbie, angry and hurt. "Aren't we friends? You've been growing more and more distant from me, Deb. When we go to the Black Rose, we don't talk anymore. You've been keeping to yourself at lunch—"

In other words, I'm becoming a perfect demon snack. When did that happen? Debbie began to giggle hysterically.

Sheila grabbed hold of her, and shook her so her teeth rattled. "What the Hell is wrong with you? Is it Amanda? That she's still missing?"

Debbie lost it, her hysteria breaking down into tears. Sheila stopped shaking her and hugged her close, smoothing her hair as she sobbed.

After a few minutes, Debbie pulled herself together, and went to push Sheila away. But Sheila pulled her in close instead, kissing her with the same passion she did everything else. Debbie pushed at her gently, finally breaking the kiss.

"I'm sorry," Sheila said, biting her lip and looking away.

"I know how you feel," Debbie said haltingly, rubbing at her eyes. "About me. I've known for a while. That's some of why I pulled away from you. But I'm also going through something that has nothing to do with you." She paused. "I'm bound to a demon."

"What's the asshole's name," Sheila said angrily. "If he's hurting you—"

"Not a man acting brutally, but a real demon," Debbie said. She grabbed her keys. "Come with me, and I'll tell you everything. But I'm not talking about it here."

Her friend stared at her for a few moments in silence. "Let me close down my computer. I'll meet you in the garage in ten minutes," Sheila said quickly, heading for the door.

* * * *

"That is the craziest story I ever heard," Sheila said three hours later, knocking back her third scotch. "If it wasn't you telling me, Deb, I'd say you were lying."

"It's all real," Debbie said, sipping her drink. Wrong or right, telling Sheila had taken a huge weight off her shoulders. "The worse thing is I don't feel that badly about what I've done. I know I should, but I don't."

"You must feel a little bit bad, or you wouldn't have gone to pieces in your office earlier," Sheila corrected. She glanced at Debbie. "Can I meet him?"

"He's not a pet."

"Can I? Please?"

"I'd think you were straight if I didn't know better," Debbie said darkly, taking a long swallow.

"I'm bi, actually," Sheila said, sounding shy for the first time Debbie could remember. "I don't usually have a thing for women. At least, I haven't for a long time. But I really like you, Debbie." She put down her glass, refilling it, then Debbie's. "But I already knew you weren't into me that way. And that's okay. I'm happy being your friend. We don't have to be more."

"You're sure?" Debbie asked. "That kiss was pretty passionate."

"I wanted it to be," Sheila said with a grin. "I knew it was probably the only one I was going to get."

Both of them smiled, then clinked glasses, and drank.

"So, can I meet him?" Sheila prodded.

"Shaker!" Debbie called loudly.

The demon appeared, inclining his head politely to a gaping Sheila, as if he met Debbie's friends every night of the week. "I am here, Mistress. And I see you've included your good friend this evening. Are we to have a threesome?"

Sheila choked on her drink, as Debbie gave Shaker slitted eyes. "No, we are not doing anything of the sort. But I do have a question for you, Shaker. How does one go about getting a demon?"

"Sharing tales of me, I see," Shaker said with a lecherous grin. "And

54

the little lady wants a little demon action of her own. It can easily be arranged, Mistress."

"Wait!" Sheila croaked out. "I didn't say I wanted a demon of my own!"

"But don't you?" Debbie said, standing unsteadily and moving to Shaker. She flipped up his loincloth, exposing him to Sheila, who went into a chocking spasm again. Debbie lowered Shaker's loincloth, then put her well-manicured hand on his red tinged muscular arm. Shaker looked over at her with a sultry look.

All I have to do is tell him what I want and he'll do it. And God, she wanted him to.

Sheila's eyes were locked on Shaker. "Say I did want a demon of my own," she said slowly. "What do I do? Find some book on demons and summon one?"

"Not recommended," Shaker said easily, crossing to Sheila and offering a taloned hand. She gave it to him, and he helped her stand. "There's no telling what you might end up with. All demons are not equal."

"Say I wanted one like you," Sheila said, some of her usual forthrightness coming back into her bearing. "Same power, same knowledge, same loyalty, same personality. Can you hook me up, for a fee?"

"No fee required," Shaker said. He kissed her hand. "Any friend of Debbie's deserves—"

"No bullshit," Sheila stated, pulling her hand out of his grip. "Not one drop. What are you getting out of this?"

Shaker eyed her for a moment, then nodded. "All right. The truth is hooking up a demon with a human who wants to bind with him—and has the guts for actually doing what is needed, which is rare—is an enormous favor to the demon. Most of the bindings that take place bust within a year. Much of that is human error, in not being careful enough with the potential power. The rest is demon error, in running amok in the human world after being cooped up in Hell." He glanced over at Debbie. "I don't pick my humans lightly, and I know how to operate without attracting undue attention. I have two friends who I think would interest you, and last I knew, both were unattached. If my Mistress is amenable,

I'd ask you to accompany us to the festival we plan on attending in two weeks. You can sample both of the potentials, and make your choice."

Sheila nodded. "Say I do pick one of them. Will there be a problem between them and you?"

"What do you mean?" Shaker asked.

"You're friends with them now, but does that change?" Sheila explained. "Say I told them to fight with you. Wouldn't they have to? And where would Debbie and I be if the two of you have a fight?"

Shaker nodded, respect in his red eyes. "You'll make a fine Mistress, Sheila. Yes, what you say can happen—and does, which is another way that these bindings end badly. I would not pick someone who would cause trouble down the line—either for Debbie or myself. It goes without saying that they have to work well with all three of us. If you decide to bind them, then we'll be something like a quartet that must work well together."

Debbie blinked, trying to clear her alcohol-fogged mind. "No foursomes."

Sheila nodded. "I understand. Yes, I'd like to meet your friend, Shaker."

Shaker turned to Debbie. "On your command, Mistress."

Debbie nodded, sitting down heavily.

Shaker covered her up with several lap robes, then kissed her softly on the cheek. Debbie fell into sleep listening to Sheila and Shaker talking.

* * * *

The next morning Debbie awoke in her bed. She was naked beneath the sheets. She turned to look for Shaker, but he wasn't there.

Debbie called in sick to work, took a long hot shower, then dressed. She went into the kitchen, and fixed herself some breakfast. After eating, she went in search of Sheila.

Her friend was in the guest bedroom, sleeping. Debbie went to her, nudging her awake.

"Ah," Sheila said, stretching happily. "Good morning. Hope you don't mind I stayed over."

"And obviously not alone," Debbie said, jealousy in her tone. "I take

56

you had sex with him?"

Sheila nodded, then bit her lip. "I hope that was okay? He said that you had not asked him for exclusivity, so it was permitted. Those were the words he used."

Something I will be remedying before the day is over. "He's right," Debbie said, plopping down on the bed. "I never asked him for exclusivity."

"Are you mad?" Sheila pressed. "I didn't want to meet his friend until I had an idea of what I was signing up for. 'Try it before you buy it' has always been my motto."

"I'm not mad," Debbie said. "I guess I'm not sure how to feel. There isn't a category I can put Shaker into, really. He isn't a boyfriend, but he isn't just a lover, either."

Sheila sat bolt upright, clutching the sheet around her. "You got him to save Pandora?"

Debbie nodded. "I thought I told you that."

"You must have glossed over that part," Sheila said. "You told me all the things he did to help us, and how you met. But I thought the sexual aspect was always there."

"Maybe it was," Debbie mused, pushing back a lock of her hair. "Maybe I just never realized it until now."

"Sexual attraction is like that sometimes," Sheila teased. Then she looked at the clock. "Holy shit! We are so late!"

"Call in, then get some sleep," Debbie said, handing her the phone. "You've got permission for the day off."

* * * *

"I'm nervous," Debbie whispered to Sheila. "And this outfit feels so odd."

Per Shaker's instructions, both of the women were dressed in long flowing gossamer type gowns that opened in the front. Each outfit had an underlayer of silky material rendering the cloth non-transparent. The style resembled a bathrobe, and covered them from head to foot.

"All humans will be wearing one, and most demons, also," Shaker reassured her. He put his arm around her. "Come, Mistress."

They strolled into the large field through simple gates of wood.

Everywhere there were demons, though most that Debbie could see did not have hooves or fur. They looked human in fact, except for their reddish skin, their black horns, and their taloned hands. Some were naked, though most were dressed like she and Sheila were. There were also a few humans, also dressed in the same robes.

"What should we do?" Sheila asked Shaker.

He pointed to a small area of tables and chairs. Nearby was a bar of sorts, with bottles and a demon dressed as a Chippendale dancer. "Take a seat at one of the tables. I'll go get us a bottle."

Sheila and Debbie chose a table and sat down, looking around uneasily. "It's not the orgy I expected," Sheila said, sounding a little disappointed. "Everyone looks so relaxed."

"If you attended orgies for decades as a matter of course," Shaker said, sitting down between them with a platter of food, a bottle and three glasses, "You would rarely leap into another with enthusiasm without a chance to get to know your partners. These parties are a chance for demons to do the things we often don't get a chance to do."

"Such as?" Debbie prodded.

"Drink, talk, and not have to do anything resembling a performance," Shaker said, pouring the wine.

"Wait," Debbie said, alarmed. "This bottle is the same as the one you had last New Year's—"

"This winery serves several vintages," Shaker said, continuing to pour. "This one is purely alcohol, Mistress."

"I can't wait until I have my own demon to call me Mistress," Sheila said eagerly, raising a glass. "To new beginnings!"

They all toasted and drank.

Debbie had wondered originally if she'd have fun at this. Shaker hadn't gone into a lot of detail about the evening, only said that other demons would be there. But the evening progressed just as he described, with easy banter, jokes, discussions of length on all sorts of subjects, and several bottles of wine. The food was good, though Debbie felt a bit bad on eating it, as Shaker could not partake. It was pure comfort food: cheese fries, donuts, cookie dough, ice cream, chocolates of all types, popcorn, cotton candy, and other snacky stuff like cheese, crackers and fruit. The wine was excellent, also: some kind of full fruity vintage with a long zap of a finish.

Sometime in the fourth hour, Shaker stopped in mid-joke and waved. "Over here, boys."

Debbie turned to see two men striding up, one tall and blond, the other short and dark. The tall blond one was handsome, and dressed in a white robe in the style of theirs. The short man was dressed in a black T-shirt and jeans, his expression sullen. As they walked closer, Debbie began to make out conversation.

"I don't know why you drag me to these damn things, Dev. I told you I'm not joining in any fucking deviant demon games—"

"Hush, Lash," the tall man said chidingly. "Shaker, it's good to see you." He turned to Debbie and Sheila, who were looking at him lustily. "Enchanté, my dears. Which one of you is Debbie?"

Debbie smiled, even as she felt Sheila's jealous look. "I am. It's good to meet you, Mr.—?"

"Call me Dev, my dear," the man said, kissing her hand with his lips. "We can be casual, I hope?"

The shock of his cold skin after the heat of Shaker's touch startled Debbie. "You're not a demon."

"You picked a bright one, didn't you?" Lash said mockingly to Shaker, who glowered at him.

"Please forgive my companion," Dev said charmingly. "He's quite out of sorts. Alas, we can only stay for a brief time. But I did want to meet you, Debbie."

"Who are you?" Sheila asked boldly of Dev, looking him up and down. "Debbie's right, you're too pale for a demon. Are you bound to one?"

Dev smiled. "And you are?"

"My name is Sheila." She extended her hand, which Dev obediently took and kissed as he had Debbie's. "But you didn't answer my question."

Dev leaned in close to Sheila, breathing deeply.

Debbie watched him uneasily. *Was he actually smelling her? Why?*

Dev leaned back. "I take it you've come here for an audition of sorts. Don't be hasty to choose, my dear. There are many demons here who would give their left horn for you to be their Mistress." He winked

59

at her. "If not something else more near and dear."

"Harp and Song are meeting us," Shaker said, his tone oddly firm, as if there was no room for discussion. Sheila and Debbie remained silent.

Dev nodded. "Probably the best of the lot," he agreed. "Either would make a fine match for this lovely girl." He shot a quick smile to the women. "I must go. Have a good time. Adieu."

He headed off. The man called Lash chuckled evilly as he looked at Debbie and Sheila, then followed him. They were soon lost in the crowd, which had swelled to double the size it had been at the threesome's arrival a few hours ago.

"Ah!" Shaker said, scanning the group. "Song! Song! Over here!"

A tall, thin woman strode up, followed by a lithe man. There was a similarity between them of facial features, as if they were possibly related. "Good to see you," the man said, taking Shaker's hand. He turned to the two women. "Now which one of you is Sheila?"

He isn't really handsome, but his sharp features are intriguing. Which will Sheila pick? "This is Sheila," Debbie said, glancing at her friend. "I'm Debbie."

"We are indebted to you for this chance," the woman said to Debbie, genuflecting slightly. The man did the same. Debbie nodded, unsure what else to do.

Shaker stood, holding out his hand to Debbie. "Shall we dance, Mistress? Let's leave them to get acquainted."

Debbie was unsure about leaving her friend, but Sheila was already talking to the man and the woman at the table, getting drinks. "Just one," she said, taking her demon's hand.

Shaker led her to the dance floor. A team of demons had taken seats behind large drums, and they were pounding out a primal rhythm, the notes bold and cloying in the sweet twilight air. Shaker and she danced, cavorting happily to the music, the beats faster and faster. Finally, Debbie motioned to Shaker, and they sank down at a nearby table, both of them breathing hard.

"Are you enjoying yourself?" Shaker asked.

Debbie nodded, then glanced over where Sheila had been sitting. Her friend was gone.

Alarmed, Debbie jumped to her feet, and made a beeline for the table, looking everywhere for her friend. She was about to yell for Sheila when Shaker grasped her arm. "There's no need to panic," he said. "I can guess where they are. Come."

Shaker lead Debbie through the crowd to the other side. A path led into the forest, lighted with small glowing orbs that looked as if they were floating on the breeze. Shaker headed down it, and Debbie followed him looking at the lights hovering in the air. "Are they magic?" she asked.

Shaker nodded. "Simple magic. If you'd like one for a night light, I can make one for you."

They came to a clearing. Set up in the center was a large tent, several lights on inside. Moaning and cries of pleasure sounded loud intermittently from within, shapes moving in rhythm.

"There," Shaker said, pointing not to the tent, but past it. On a knoll by a large stone set into the ground were several couples of varying genders. Sheila was among them, standing with the two demons that Shaker had introduced her to earlier. One by one, each couple went to the stone and laid one of their hands on it, clasping the hand of their partner in the other. Then they kissed, and walked toward the tent hand in hand.

"What are they doing?" Debbie whispered.

"Binding," Shaker said just as quietly. "Then consummating the tie in flesh in the tent beyond. Neither is really necessary for the bind to work, but both our races do like their rituals." He turned to Debbie. "We can do it ourselves if you wish to, Mistress."

Debbie shook her head, watching Sheila ascend to the stone. To her surprise, both the man and the woman came to stand beside her friend, placing their hands on the stone, and joining their free hand with hers.

"She's taking both of them," Shaker said approvingly. "Sheila does have the mettle for it." He glanced at Debbie. "And that's good for us, too. Song and Harp are both solid workers. They'll be an asset to Pandora, and to us, as well as to Sheila."

Debbie nodded, watching Sheila walk to the tent hand in hand with her two new demons. As much as she was pleased that her friend was now protected like she was, Debbie also felt like she had fallen into deep black water that was about to close over her head.

Chapter Five

~ May ~

"Your weekly rose delivery," Kaitlin said pleasantly, delivering the multihued bouquet to Debbie's desk. She handed the card to Debbie, then went back to her office.

"Thank you, Kaitlin," Debbie said, sparing a smile for her new secretary as she shut the office door. Then she picked the sealed card off the flowers and opened it up.

As usual, Henry had asked that she join him for dinner. Their last few had been enjoyable enough, discussing movies and films of the last few decades. But while he obviously wanted more than the chaste kiss she allowed him at her front door at the close of each evening, Debbie was unsure what she wanted. Shaker spent most nights at her house now, in her bed. He had accepted her order of exclusivity with a smile and a nod, no arguments. *So what was she supposed to do, tell him to get lost for a night so she could bed Henry?*

Debbie rubbed her eyes, then called for Sheila. Five minutes later, her friend was in her office, seating herself in the office chair.

"And how are you this fine morning?" Sheila practically sang. "I'm feeling so good I could burst out in song."

"Please don't," Debbie said with a snort. "Though I am happy you're happy. These last few weeks I've really noticed it, Sheila. You were always optimistic before. But you seem so much happier now."

"And you know why," Sheila said with a wicked grin. "Those two

62

are just wonderful, Debbie. I'm not alone anymore. And we get along really well."

"I'm glad," Debbie replied absently.

Sheila's eyes narrowed. "But?"

"But nothing," Debbie said quickly. She passed a report to Sheila. "Well, honestly, this is what's the matter. *Smoke and Ashes* is still over budget. I know you've worked really hard and cut corners, even got us some amazing deals. But sales from *Tinderbox* are slowing down, and there's going to be a lapse in revenue until that hits DVD and Movies on Demand. I don't want to delay the film, but I'm not sure what else to do. We have no petty cash to spare."

Sheila paged through the report. "What about *Absolution*?"

Debbie shook her head. "We made that on a shoestring to begin with, and we've stopped production on it for now, cutting expenses to the bone. I don't know where else to cut. I'm faced with layoffs or pushing back the picture." She grimaced. "If only *Hell's Gate* hadn't been delayed. But that asshole at the ratings board still refuses to budge on his R-rating."

"I bet I can get him to budge," Sheila said darkly. "With a little help, of course."

Debbie looked at her searchingly. "Are you sure that's wise?"

"What did we get our...um... help for, unless it's to use for these kinds of circumstances?" Sheila responded, standing. "Let me try. I'll be discreet."

"Okay," Debbie said, nodding. "Give it a shot."

Sheila walked out, and Debbie went back to her pile of paperwork.

Later in the week, Henry joined Debbie for dinner at Andy's. They made polite conversation until Henry put down his fork mid-sentence. "What's wrong, Debbie? You've been distant all evening."

Debbie looked at him, then decided that Henry was likely privy already to anything she was going to reveal about Pandora. She told him about her cash flow problem, leaving out Sheila's plan to solve it in house.

Henry asked a few more questions, then changed the subject. An hour later as they were eating dessert, he abruptly changed it back. "Back to your cash-flow problems...what about Pandora Promotions, the former Panko Promos?"

Debbie hadn't done much with the company since acquiring it, other than assign Jeremy to oversee it. "It's turning a profit, but not much of one, Henry. I was going to look into selling it next quarter, as my team tells me we don't really need a promotions company just for our own products. And we aren't set up right now to really go after other clients to grow the business to make the company more profitable."

"Why not sell it now?" Henry said. "I can think of two other corporations that would be interested, neither of them film related." He quoted a figure that Debbie thought overly large. "Would that be enough to see you through?"

Debbie nodded. "More than enough to see us through. But what kind of fee would you want, Henry? There would be a good deal of paperwork involved. At least, there was when I initially bought the company from Dante."

"I'm sure we could come to some agreeable figure," Henry said, touching Debbie's hand gently. "I give special rates for friends."

Debbie smiled back at him, her thoughts churning on what to do.

* * * *

Later that night in bed, Debbie told Shaker about her day. He listened, then nodded at Sheila's suggestion. "Harp and Song will be able to sway him," he said, massaging Debbie's feet. "Those two have a wealth of magic between them, especially with illusions."

Debbie looked over at Shaker, watching his taloned hands skillfully caress her feet. "What about you? What magic do you know?"

"A fair amount," he answered. "My offer of a glow ball is still open, if you desire one for a night light."

"How about turning lead into gold," Debbie said dejectedly. "Even if I could get *Hell's Gate* into theaters tomorrow, I'd still need funds to see us through July."

"What you need is an investor or two," Shaker suggested. "A few powerful friends can make all the difference." He kissed her toes, then crawled up the bed to take her in his arms. "I might know a friend or two I could recommend."

Debbie shook her head. "Investors usually want some control over the company. That's exactly what Titan is trying for, Shaker. I don't want to compromise the kinds of films Pandora makes."

"These investors won't want to call the shots, trust me," Shaker replied. "They're more behind-the-scenes kind of people."

Debbie made a face. "Are they demons, too?"

"No," Shaker said. "We've got quite enough demons at Pandora already, real and fake." He smiled. "In fact, I was going to suggest that Pandora do something to recognize that. Maybe have a party on New Year's celebrating the Year of the Demon. All of your films since you took control feature at least one."

Debbie started to laugh at his humor, then stopped. *Shaker was right. Demons did appear in all Pandora films this year.*

Hell's Gate was a horror/action movie featuring a self-sacrificing priest taking on the legions of hell for a little girl's soul. *Tinderbox* had detailed a small town that was ripped apart by a demon's machinations of their deepest fears and desires. *Absolution* was a man's journey to forgiveness for his wife for having an affair with his brother, with a demon who appeared now and again to try to push him to murdering her instead.

And the crown jewel, *Smoke and Ashes*, was the story of a demon-possessed dead man's ride to vengeance against the group of men who had brutally killed him and his family. Once the hero had justice, he vowed to take his own life to join his loved ones. Instead at the movie's end, the demon convinced him to use his power to continue to fight the forces of evil. Debbie had seen the script for what it was: a series beginning. She'd optioned two sequels from the writer when she bought the script.

"I could probably arrange some spectacular events for a New Year's celebration," Shaker added. "There are many demons who are pleased with what you've done for us that would be happy to help out, free of charge."

Debbie stared at him. "What?"

"Even as the villain, having demons up on the silver screen is good publicity. I had several demons contact me in the last few weeks, telling me to let them know if I—and by virtue of association, you—needed anything done." He smiled. "It's good to have favors owed."

The idea was strange, but Shaker was right that it would be fabulous publicity. "Do what you can to set up something spectacular," Debbie said, nodding slowly. "I'll talk to Sheila and get a venue booked."

"Of course," Shaker said. "Now I must broach the subject of sustenance again—"

"Already?" Sheila said, taken aback.

Shaker laughed. "Just being proactive, Mistress. I thought I should give you more lead time this period. Tell me by August. That is close enough, barring some injury."

Debbie nodded absently, her mind already at work on possible choices.

Shaker leaned up on one arm and looked down at her. "If you want to bed Henry, mistress, you have only to say so."

Debbie snapped out of her thoughts, then stretched and sighed. "I don't know if I want to. I don't know if I can trust him. And even if I could…how would it work?"

"Pretty simply," Shaker said, lying down on his back. "You call me when you need me for something, and I'll be out of the way the rest of the time."

Debbie sat up, then wrapped a blanket around her shoulders.

Shaker touched her thigh gently. "Are you cold? I'm surprised."

"No," Debbie said, pushing her hair back from her face. *God, it was getting long.* She made a mental note next month to take that option at the Black Rose instead of the facial. She turned to look at Shaker. "It's because I'm not cold. Shaker, the longer this goes on between us, the weirder I feel about it."

Shaker put his hands behind his head, his face bemused. "That's a normal feeling, Mistress."

Debbie threw up her hands, exasperated. 'But that's just it! None of my life is normal anymore! I'm having sex with a demon and going to pagan orgies—"

"Demon orgies," Shaker corrected. "Paganism is a faith all its own."

"—and you're killing people and eating them, and acting like it's just another day—"

Shaker sat up, taking her hand in his large hot ones. He cupped it in his palms. "Mistress, this is how I live. To me, this is just another day."

He kissed her hands gently in turn. "It's just another year of an existence that varies so little it sometimes seems monotonous." He looked up at her, his red eyes serious. "But this year so far…it's a good one, don't you think?"

Debbie bit her lip, looking away.

"You have your company. You have a good friend, you have a love interest—" His tone lightened. "—and you've got one of the best lovers in existence. That's not a bad life to be leading."

Debbie smiled faintly. "And who said demons didn't have big egos?"

"That's not all we possess of size," Shaker rumbled, taking her in his arms and kissing her gently.

* * * *

The next day, Sheila came into the office, her expression hard. She stood there, fuming.

Debbie grimaced, leaning back in her chair with her pen tapping a staccato on the desktop. "So the ratings guy said no?"

"He said yes, with a little convincing," Sheila retorted, flopping into the chair opposite. "But he's going to need a week to change his paperwork, or so said Harp. Because the man was so against the PG-13 rating, it's going to take a while to fix his movie labels of the last few months to reflect his new ideals."

"He's going to change others?" Debbie's brow furrowed. "Why not just change the one rating for us?"

"Because it would be obvious we did something. We really need that rating, but we really don't need anyone to take notice. If he just changes *Hell's Gate*, someone will eventually see it as an aberration compared with his usual reviews. Song and Harp both were in agreement that we want no one to think anything is amiss."

Shaker was right. Those two would be valuable assets. Debbie nodded approvingly. "Smart. Very smart. Can you take care of it?"

Sheila nodded, then looked down at Debbie's stack of paperwork. "Did you find me some cash?"

"Maybe." Debbie detailed out both Henry's plan for the sale of the promo company, and also Shaker's suggestion of investors.

Shelia listened to both, then shrugged. "I'm with you on investors," she said. "They usually want to strip all the originality out of a picture, and replace it with something cookie cutter that they hope will sell. They also usually aren't afraid to use their grip on the budget to get their way. But I also don't like the idea of selling any part of Pandora." She paused. "Do we have to do one of them? Can't we wait for revenue from *Hell's Gate*?"

Debbie shook her head. "We can't count on that. You know that a large majority of the films made don't recoup their production costs."

"*Hell's Gate* will. And *Smoke and Ashes* defiantly will. Everyone likes the wronged hero out for a little payback."

"I agree, but we can't spend what we don't have," Debbie said flatly. "And the revenue from *Hell's Gate*, if it's a hit, won't be in time. Look, I care what you think, Sheila. I want us to be together on this decision. Which do you want to try?"

"A choice of evils," Sheila quipped. "Fine. If we're going to be evil, we might as well go all the way. Let's take a look at Shaker's investors. And let's also see the offer Henry can make us for the promo division. Formally, as in on paper."

"All right," Debbie said. "Give my thanks to Harp and Song." She put down her pen, glancing over at Sheila. "Have you paid either of them your favor yet?"

"What favor?" Sheila asked quizzically.

Debbie struggled awkwardly trying to find words that weren't horrible. "Have you fed them?" Debbie finally said in a strangled tone.

"Oh!" Sheila said, blinking rapidly. "That. Yes. They explained the parameters, and said it needed to be regularly, but not every month. I take it you've done yours?"

Debbie nodded. "It was hard for me to do. And I've got to do it again soon. Any advice?"

"Do it fast, and at random," Sheila said confidently. "Thinking about it just makes you feel guilty. At least that's what I did."

Debbie made a face. "Maybe I'll try that this time."

Sheila stood. "Do you need anything else? I'm auditioning actors to play the part of the fallen priest in *Smoke and Ashes* in ten minutes."

"Go on," Debbie said, picking up the phone to call Henry.

A Good Year

* * * *

"So what do you think?" Henry said to Debbie on Saturday over their weekly dinner. "I haven't heard a word about my proposal all week."

"I'm on the fence," Debbie admitted, sipping her wine. She set the glass down. "While I know that the price you're offering for Pandora Promos is generous compared to the price I paid Dante to buy it, I'm not sure I want to sell it to Titan."

"They'll give you the best price," Henry replied evenly. "The economy is not the best, Deb. I checked around, and their price is the best I could do without Titan suspecting anything. You can sell to one of the other companies that put in offers, but you're going to get at least 10K less in revenue…and Titan will take notice."

"I know that," Debbie said, clasping his hand. "I'm grateful, Henry, really. But I'm still thinking it over."

Henry nodded, then squeezed her hand. "Fair enough. But I do have another question I want you to answer." He paused. "Do you want more than what we have now?"

Debbie tried not to fidget, feeling her stomach clench. *Be calm! You knew this was coming.*

"Because I do," Henry continued. "But I don't want to go on seeing you on Saturday nights any longer if you don't really think we have a future together. Tell me the truth, Debbie."

Be calm and breathe. Don't squirm! Don't look away! Presentation face, quick! Debbie collected herself with effort, and managed a smile. "I like being with you, P—" Debbie stopped short, utterly horrified that she'd been about to call Henry by her dead lover's name. She flushed, looking away.

Henry grabbed her hand. "Do you want more than this?"

Look at him and take control of this situation now, said a commanding voice from within Debbie. She straightened, then looked into Henry's eyes and nodded.

His face relaxed, beaming happily. "I'm so glad, Debbie. I really am." He turned, calling for the waiter.

Debbie took a deep breath, then downed the rest of her wine, thinking frantically.

* * * *

When Henry saw her home that night, he didn't step away and leave as he usually did after she kissed him goodnight. Instead, he held her. "May I come in tonight?" he asked gently. "I don't want to leave yet."

Debbie smiled faintly, then said the words she'd mentally rehearsed all though dessert. "I'm sorry, but I can't let you, Henry."

Henry blinked in surprise at her refusal. "Why not?"

Debbie wiped the fake smile off her face, and let some of her real anguish show through. "The last man I was involved with was…he was married, Henry. It ended badly. And I swore after that I wasn't going to have any casual love affairs—"

"This isn't casual," Henry persisted. "You must know that, Debbie. I'm very serious about you."

"I'm not saying this to hurt you," Debbie said, flushing again. "I just made a promise to myself that I wasn't going to leap into any more relationships until I was absolutely ready. And I'm not." She touched his cheek gently. "But I will be soon, Henry. Please give me a little more time."

Henry looked disgruntled, but he nodded. "I understand." He stepped back, his smile gone. "I'll call you." He walked away quickly to his car.

He'd known I was lying to him. It was all over his face.

Debbie fumbled for her keys, and shoved them into the lock, nearly breaking them off in her haste to get inside. She shut the door hard, the roar of Henry's car driving away loud in her ears. The finality of it broke something inside her and she fell against the door, beginning to sob. Her legs buckled.

Shaker's arms materialized around her before she hit the floor. "Shh, Mistress. I'm here."

"I can't do this," Debbie sobbed. "I can't do this anymore, Shaker."

"Shh," Shaker said, picking her up in his arms. He kicked the door shut with his hoof, then carried her into her bed, laying her down. He undressed her to her underwear, then pulled the blankets over her, flipping on the air conditioning.

70

"Leave me alone," Debbie cried. "Leave me alone tonight."

Shaker paused, then turned to her. "Are you sure, Mistress?"

Debbie sobbed, and didn't answer.

Shaker moved to the door, then turned to her, his red eyes glowing in the gloom. "Get some sleep," he said, flipping off the light. "Tomorrow is another day."

Chapter Six

~ June ~

Debbie's phone buzzed abruptly, startling her. She hit the intercom button. "Yes, Kaitlin?"

"There is a Mrs. Triss here to see you."

"Please tell him there are no openings at this time."

"*Mrs.* Triss," her new secretary repeated. "I'm not sure who you think I meant, but this woman says that she has an appointment with you. Didn't you say you had someone coming for a ten o'clock meeting today?"

This couldn't be Shaker's investor? She fumbled for her appointment book. There in big red letters in Shaker's scrawled handwriting was the name "Mrs. T" with the time of ten a.m. for that day. He'd blocked off a half hour.

"Mrs. Deal?"

Fuck! "Please show her in."

Debbie grabbed her files on Pandora's financial needs and her presentation packet as Kaitlin showed an elderly well-dressed woman into the office. "Lady" was the only term Debbie could apply to the woman. Mrs. Triss was sleek and elegant as a swan in tailored clothes, perfect makeup, and silvery white hair.

Debbie groaned inwardly, remembering she had yet to get a haircut. *This week, definitely.* She stood, offering her hand. "I'm very glad to meet you."

"Will you need anything?" Kaitlin asked.

"No," Debbie said, gesturing for Mrs. Triss to sit. "But please hold all my calls, Kaitlin."

Kaitlin nodded, and shut the door. Debbie turned back to Mrs. Triss, who was staring at her. The unwavering gaze made Debbie's skin crawl, but she forced a smile. "It's good to meet you," she said, extending her hand.

"Sit down," Mrs. Triss said regally. "I didn't come here for B.S., Ms. Deal. Shaker said you had a worthwhile opportunity. At least, he convinced my husband of that."

Was this Rack's wife? It couldn't be. He would be forty-odd years younger. Maybe Rack was her son or grandson? "Do I know your husband?"

Mrs. Triss smiled darkly. "I believe you do, Debbie. You turned him down for a job he wanted more than anything." She plucked the presentation off Debbie's desk, setting it on her lap. "He would have incinerated you for that, except for your bond with Shaker."

"Who are you?" Debbie asked harshly. "And what do you really want?"

Mrs. Triss looked up, then tossed down the presentation on Debbie's desk. "Forgive me," she said a little less frostily. "My ability to coexist with the rest of the human race seems to ebb each year. As for what I want and who I am, you already know that. I'm here to invest."

"Who are you?" Debbie repeated. "Mrs. Triss—a.k.a. Rack's—wife?"

Mrs. Triss looked stunned, then let out a peal of laughter. "He told you his real name," she said. "Stands to reason. He really did want that job in acquisitions."

"He'd have had it, if he hadn't been so odd," Debbie retorted. "He did have the most experience."

Mrs. Triss nodded. "Which is why I don't need to see your presentation, Mrs. Deal, though I'm sure it's persuasive. Rack says this is a good opportunity. And in sixty years, he's never steered me wrong."

The bad feeling in Rack's interview. His odd behavior. Her crack about incineration. "He's a demon."

Mrs. Triss nodded. "You might have recognized that, if you'd been a bit more experienced." She winked. "But that will come in time."

Debbie sat down, so many questions churning in her mind she wasn't sure what to ask first.

Mrs. Triss rose from her chair, and put a small black business card on Debbie's desk. "If you send me the paperwork, I'll return it promptly." She smiled, then extended her hand. "It's good to be working with you, Mrs. Deal."

Debbie stood, but didn't put out her hand. "Would you like to have lunch? To celebrate our deal? My treat."

Mrs. Triss tilted her head slightly, studying her. "A little early for lunch, don't you think?"

"No," Debbie said, grabbing her purse. "I know a great place."

* * * *

Mrs. Triss let out another huge peal of laughter, drawing more grumpy looks from the other patrons at Andy's. "He really said that? 'That's not all we possess of size?'" She dissolved into laughter.

"Yes!" Debbie laughed with her, then poured them both another glass of wine, finishing the bottle. She wiped at her eyes with her napkin, then sipped her wine.

Mrs. Triss sipped her wine, then set the glass down. She motioned for a waiter.

"Did you want dessert?" Debbie asked with a smile, eating the last of her salad. "They have some great ones here."

"No," Mrs. Triss said. "I want another vintage." She took the proffered wine list from the waiter, then pointed to the very bottom of it. The waiter nodded, then left.

Mrs. Triss passed the list to Debbie, who about choked on her forkful of lettuce. The wine the woman had chosen was three hundred dollars!

"No need to look appalled, Mrs. Deal," Mrs. Triss said. "I'm treating for this."

I should have corrected her the first time she addressed me as "Mrs." "There's no 'Mrs.', Mrs. Triss," Debbie explained patiently. "It's Ms."

"In time, it might be easier if you were Mrs.," the lady replied. "It discourages suitors. Lord knows they tend to foul things up."

"Mrs. Triss," Debbie amended. "May I call you by your first name?"

"You may not," Mrs. Triss said politely. "Names have power, girl. But you can just call me Triss, if you like. That was a name I used once."

She's as wacky as her demon husband. Keep calm and get what info you can. "You seem to know a lot about demons. Is there anything you can tell me?"

"Not to trust them," Mrs. Triss said, then tittered.

The waiter brought the wine, and poured it. Debbie took the bottle, her eyes round. It was the same brand that Shaker had used at the party...and before that, on Paul.

"Cheers," Mrs. Triss said, raising her glass.

Debbie raised hers, but though she smiled, her eyes were cold. "You first."

"Ah," Mrs. Triss said, setting down her glass. "Now there is a glimmer of intelligence. I knew you must have it, if you were Shaker's."

"It's he who belongs to me," Debbie corrected.

"You belong to each other," the lady amended. "If he dies in the flesh, you'll die, too. But if you die, he can live again. That is something to remember, Ms. Deal. Because you're both headed to the same place now, if the worst happens."

Debbie put down her glass. "I don't need lofty warnings of what I already know. Tell me something I don't know and make yourself useful."

A waiter heard her upset tone, and hurried over. "Is something wrong with the wine?"

"No," Mrs. Triss said sharply. "Now go away and don't disturb us until we motion for you."

The waiter hurried away, shaken.

Mrs. Triss faced Debbie. "You want information? Fine. Here's your first lesson. Everything you know, everything you feel, everything you see...Shaker has been privy to all that, from the very beginning."

Debbie blinked, confused. "He was with me and invisible?"

"He was looking through your eyes. They like to do that, to keep an eye on you. You are essentially possessed, after a fashion. He could make your voice, your body, your will his own if he wanted."

"Why?"

"Defense, first and foremost. If you're threatened, you probably couldn't fight your way out of a paper bag. But Shaker could move you to block an attack. Not that they do that often. They can feel our pain, as I've said. It attracts them." She smiled again nastily. "Demons like pain, especially their Mistress's pain."

"I don't believe you," Debbie whispered.

"Mark my words," Mrs. Triss said. "You either control your demon, or they control you. There can be a partnership, sure. But there is always a leader and a follower. Which are you?"

"Which are you?" Debbie countered.

Mrs. Triss smiled, then raised her glass. "I'm going to like you very much, Ms. Deal." She sipped her wine, then put down the glass.

Debbie watched her carefully.

"You can drink it." Mrs. Triss took another of her black cards out of her purse, and passed it to Debbie. "I know you didn't look at it in your office, but I'm sure you'll recognize the crest."

Debbie picked up the card and studied the Celtic crest. Its interwoven demonic figures, thin and winged, matched the bottle's label. "You make this wine."

"Many vintages," Mrs. Triss said, taking a long swallow. "Several just for private buyers."

Debbie looked at the glass, then back at her companion.

"Ask him if it's all right, if you drink it," Mrs. Triss said with a faint smile. "Call him mentally. He's bound to answer."

Shaker? Debbie thought tentatively. *Are you there?*

Yes, came the reluctant reply in her mind. The voice was not her own. It was the odd voice that had told her to get hold of herself when Henry was confessing his love.

Debbie stifled a scream, gripping the table. She grabbed for the table knife, but Mrs. Triss slapped her hand over Debbie's, holding it down with a small clang. Several patrons looked over, then resumed eating.

You've been here all along, Debbie thought frantically. *You never needed me to tell you anything that happened. That's how you knew Henry's name and had the investors ready to suggest—!*

Yes, Shaker answered. *But this is not a bad thing, Mistress. And as*

I've said before, if you wish me to block this part of the bond on occasion, it can be done. But if you are attacked while our mental link is down—as Triss mentioned—I will not be able to react instantly.

Debbie turned terrified eyes to Mrs. Triss, who grabbed her other hand that was heading for the fork. "Shaker," Mrs. Triss said under her breath. "Leave her in my care for a while. Rack can keep both of us safe for a half hour or so."

"It's your life if he doesn't," Shaker replied, the words with odd inflection coming unbidden out of Debbie's mouth. "I like this one. You or he fucks with that, you're both done."

Mrs. Triss nodded, then said in a new low voice, with a French accent, "I'll take care of them. I'll wait with them, unseen. My word."

Debbie nodded, then her rigid body collapsed back into the chair, her chest heaving. Mrs. Triss was more composed, but she also grabbed for her water glass, drinking down the entire thing.

Debbie bit her lip until blood came, trying to hold back tears.

"There, there," Mrs. Triss said, setting aside her water glass and taking Debbie's hand. "It's okay once you get used to it. And it's rarely done...only when necessary, like just now."

"I can't do this," Debbie said, dabbing at her eyes with her napkin.

"Yes, you can," Mrs. Triss said staunchly, offering a hanky from her purse. "We're going to make some fabulous movies, Ms. Deal. And I hope you'll consider putting my wine in your films, now and again." She smiled. "Any free advertising I can get is always appreciated."

Debbie blinked back more tears, then used the hanky.

"Keep it, please," the lady said. "Now I think we should head to the park across the street. It's a lovely day, and a little sunlight would cheer you." She motioned for the waiter. "Please bag that wine to go."

Debbie nodded, reaching for her purse.

* * * *

Mrs. Triss and Debbie sat on a bench in the sun for several minutes, not speaking. The wind was easy, the light was bright, the heat from the sun soaking into Debbie. She raised her face to it, wondering with sadness how long it had been since she had sat outside. *Since April? Longer?*

"Feeling better?"

Debbie turned to Mrs. Triss. "How did you begin? Did Ra…um, Mr. Triss approach you?"

Mrs. Triss smiled, then looked away. "A long story."

"I'm not going anywhere for another twenty minutes. Give me the condensed version."

Mrs. Triss nodded. "It began with a huge summer storm when I was seven. Hurricane force winds. Boats were smashed and floating in the water offshore, and many items of all kinds were floating near the shore afterwards. Lying there on the rocks was a box. It looked like a child's toy box, but it wasn't filled with toys. The things in it were real."

"What do you mean?" asked Debbie.

"There were all kinds of miniatures. Tiny tubes of paints and pens that really wrote. Tiny figures of cats and goats and insects. A shelf of various perfumes, scents that I'd never smelled, and one of makeup. But those last I paid no attention to at seven." She paused. "I should have known something was weird. Nothing was wet or broken, you see. Everything was in perfect condition."

"At first I played with the figures and the art supplies. But every time I looked in the box, I seemed to find more nooks and crannies with more hidden wonders inside. Tiny books with writing in them. Paper to draw on. Ribbons for my hair."

"The more I looked inside the box, the more I wanted to lose myself in it. It got so that my mother had to pry it away from me and keep it locked up." Mrs. Triss smiled. "She was a good one for discipline, my mother was. And her punishment worked. With distance came forgetting. I went off to boarding school that autumn with no thoughts of the box. And I didn't think about it until years later, when I came across it cleaning out her things after her death."

"I opened it on a lark, wanting to see how my adult perception would view the aged magic of my childhood. I was sure that I must have imagined so much that I remembered. But I didn't." Mrs. Triss's tone had grown haunted. "Everything was real. But more compelling…almost everything had changed."

"Gone was the artwork, the figurines, and most of the miniatures. The makeup and perfume remained of what I remembered. But now

78

there were also goblets, plates, and glasses of silver and brass." She looked up at Debbie, tears in her eyes. "They were perfect for my wedding reception, which was in three days. So I brought the box home with me."

She paused again, dabbing at her eyes.

"What happened?"

"My fiancé Raul laughed, calling me a girl playing with toys instead of a grown woman. My anger was instantaneous. I lashed out at him, and we had our first fight. But we forgave one another almost instantly."

"Our marriage was beautiful, the reception perfect. We settled into married life. But Raul's job frequently took him away. When he was gone, I often lost myself in the box for days at a time. But I was always careful to set an alarm clock for a few hours before he was due home, so that I'd have time to shower and clean up the house." Her tone was grim. "Then my twenty-first birthday came. I thought Raul had forgotten. He was scheduled to be out of town. But instead he'd planned a surprise party for me."

"I was tired and annoyed at being alone on my birthday. So I bought myself a cake—double chocolate—and was eating a slice in my pajamas and drawing with several of the miniature pens that remained. Friends started arriving. At first, I thought they were only stopping by. These were my closest friends, but they had no idea about the box, or how it was important to me. I made excuses that I was tired, and left them, going upstairs to my sitting room with my drawing."

"My closest friend Julia followed me, berating me about how I looked. She was worried. When she came into my bedroom, she saw the box. Immediately, she reached for it, and began to touch the makeup." Mrs. Triss smiled. "How thrilled she was when she saw that it had the power to make her years younger in mere seconds."

"I was furious, and took the bottle away from her, screaming at her to leave. Raul came in, grabbing and restraining me. He thought I was sick. The noise had drawn my other friends. He yelled at them to leave, to call a doctor for me. But they all ignored us. To a person, they had been ensnared by the box. Grabbing and shoving each other, they tore into it, sampling everything! I screamed at them to stop. Raul turned on me, angrier than I'd ever seen him. He said it was my fault, that I had guests, that he was tired of never having all my attention, that he might as well not have a wife!" Anger and bitterness threaded each of her words. "He was always doing that to me. Expecting me to deal with all of the duties so he could play host with Daddy's money. I yelled at him that I never wanted a party, that I hadn't wanted anyone to come, that I'd made a mistake in marrying him."

Mrs. Triss fell silent.

"What happened?" Debbie said finally.

"I killed him," Mrs. Triss said softly. "He tried to choke me, and I stabbed him with a hatpin from my vanity. When I recovered enough to stand, I looked around and saw that my friends were dead. The items from the box had killed them." She smiled faintly. "The makeup and the perfume had burned the women...they'd used it all. And the men had beaten one another to death with the goblets."

Debbie stared in horror.

"Natalie had stabbed out her own eyes with the tiny pens. She never liked makeup..."

Debbie got to her feet. *Shaker?* she called mentally. There was no answer.

"It was then that the demon who lived in the box revealed himself," Mrs. Triss finished. She looked up at Debbie. "The box—and he—were mine, you see. That's what he said. And no one would ever come between us."

A young man—the Mr. Triss that she had met months ago, a.k.a. Rack—materialized by Mrs. Triss, kneeling at her feet. "Shh, Mistress," he said softly, wiping at her tears. "Don't remember the beginning mistakes. We can't undo the past."

Debbie poised to run, trying to decide which direction to flee. Rack grasped her arm faster than she could react to avoid him.

"You killed her friends," Debbie stammered. "You killed her husband."

"He was a lout that beat her when he was home, and fucked anything in a skirt when he wasn't," the demon said viciously, looking over her. "She deserved better." He squeezed her arm until Debbie cried in pain. "And I'll thank you not to remind her again of old pain. She's suffered enough."

Shaker materialized, his taloned hand ripping Rack's hand off of Debbie. "Don't overstep yourself, child," Shaker snarled with flame-filled eyes. "This lesson hath ended."

Rack glowered, but retreated to Mrs. Triss's side, helping her to rise. She leaned on him heavily. Slowly, he walked her away through the park, until they disappeared from sight in the crowded parking lot.

"Come," Shaker said, offering her his hand. "I believe we have a lot to talk about, Mistress."

* * * *

"You lied to me."

Shaker stamped his left hoof, leaving an indentation in the kitchen's wood floor. "I can't offer up to you what you do not ask," he said for the fifth time, exasperated. "That is Hell's rule, Mistress. I cannot break it without penalty."

"That might be so," Debbie said slowly. "But I command you now as your Mistress to tell me now in a list of any and all powers that you have omitted from me. I want to know why Rack was at that interview all those months ago. I want to know who he is to you."

"Easy enough. He's an acquaintance. When he heard that you and I got together, he wanted to know if he could come and work at Pandora. He worked in film a good many years as a human, and it seemed like a good fit—"

"He was once a human?"

"Not all demons are fallen angels," Shaker said sadly. "Some are turned by curse, like we did to Paul. Others are so evil that when they die they become demons. Rack was one of the cursed ones. That box he was tied to was part of it." He smiled. "But you'll be pleased to know that with his woman's help, he was able to free himself from it—"

"I could give a flying fuck about Rack, Shaker. I want to know why you chose them as investors."

"Because they won't interfere with us," he answered, unfazed by Debbie's anger. "And because Rack was pissed off when you didn't hire him. This was a way of smoothing things over. He likes the pictures we've been making, and he wanted to be a part of that. That's all."

Debbie studied him.

"I swear, Mistress."

There was a crack of thunder, and then rain poured down outside, sheeting the windows. Neither Debbie or Shaker moved.

"Leave me tonight," Debbie said. "No eavesdropping at all. Understood?"

Shaker nodded, then disappeared.

Debbie moved to the phone, picked it up and punched in a number. "Sheila? I need you to come over. Can you?"

"Of course," Sheila said, appearing with Harp in Debbie's kitchen a few feet away before she finished speaking. Debbie let out a shriek and toppled over backwards in surprise.

Song caught her, steadying her. "You okay?"

"Send them away," Debbie said, pushing the demon away and clutching the kitchen counter.

Sheila went over to Debbie, hugging her. "What happened?"

"Send them away," Debbie repeated stonily, staring at Harp and Song. "Tell them no eavesdropping at all. Say it, Sheila."

"What she said," Sheila said, looking at Harp and Song. "I'll be here if there's an emergency."

Harp and Song glanced at one another angrily, but disappeared.

Sheila guided Debbie into the living room, and sat her down on the couch. "Want to tell me what the Hell is going on?"

"No," Debbie said reluctantly. "I really don't. But you're my best friend, Sheila. I have to…especially when it was me that got you into this."

* * * *

"And then Shaker came and made Rack back off," Debbie finished, sipping her scotch. "Then I told Shaker I needed some time and called you and you got here. Which, by the way, was accomplished how?"

"Teleportation," Sheila said proudly. "I shall never have to wake up at 5 am again to commute into Pandora. I can get up at seven, get dressed, eat a leisurely breakfast until 7:59, and be there in the blink of an eye in time for work."

"Damn you," Debbie said grumpily. "Why are your demons so forthcoming? You have all the luck."

"They didn't volunteer anything," Sheila said, finishing her shot. "I had to pry it out of them. Took me most of the first week in hour-long question and answer sessions. And they still found a way to leave a lot out. I had no idea they could look through my eyes and see what I saw. I knew they could hear me mentally if I called them, but I had no idea that they were privy to my thoughts anytime they chose to check in."

Debbie bit her lip. "You know all I know, Sheila. Is there anything you found out that I didn't?"

Sheila thought for a moment. "They can invade dreams," she said. "If you dream of Shaker, odds are he not only was in the dream with you, he instigated it."

Debbie shook her head. "No dreams so far of demons. Anything else?"

"A demon can't kill its master. But if it wants to trade up, so to speak, it can enlist another human to do the job. That human usually binds the demon once the deed is done."

God, something else new to worry about. "Why?"

"'Humans die eventually'," Sheila said grimly. "That's the excuse Harp gave. 'A demon doesn't want to get sent back to hell, so they switch out before their card gets punched.' That second phrase was from Song."

"Something to look forward to in our old age," Debbie said grimly, thinking of Mrs. Triss. "How nice."

"There is one more thing," Sheila said awkwardly. "Your demon is something of a legend."

"Well?" Debbie said after a full minute of silence. "Aren't you going to elaborate?"

Sheila fidgeted, then said "Did Shaker ever appear to you without his loincloth?"

Debbie blinked. "I've seen him naked dozens of times."

"But did he come to you naked? Appear without his cloth?"

"Once," Debbie said, nodding. "After the first favor."

Sheila looked away.

"What?"

"That loincloth he wears? It's made of human skin. Shaker takes the skin himself from the victim and tans it, so it takes a while to do. He makes a new one with every new master."

Debbie felt her gorge rising. Choking on bile, she ran for the bathroom.

* * * *

"Did you eat the entire menu at Andy's?" Sheila chided, wiping Debbie's face with the washcloth. Her friend was kneeling before the toilet bowl, pasty white and swaying. "Are you done?"

"Amanda," Debbie moaned. "I'm so sorry. I'm so sorry."

"Enough with the apologies," Sheila said, helping her friend to her feet. "She's either already moved on to Heaven, or unimpressed with your suffering and waiting for you in Hell. Either way, we've got bigger problems."

"Like?" Debbie managed.

"Like Dante," Sheila said. "He paid Pandora a visit this afternoon, waving a video tape. He's lawyered up and planning to charge you with murder."

Chapter Seven

~ July ~

"What good is having a demon if you can't do anything about a hangover?" Debbie said crossly, fixing her hair in the mirror. Shaker stood behind her leaning against the doorjamb, watching.

"Need I go over Hell's position on suffering again?" Shaker replied drolly. "If you'd let me join the party, I'd have watched over you and made sure you paced yourself—"

"Okay, enough," Debbie said, holding up her palm. She put the final touches on her hair, then turned to him. "What do we do now?"

"Take my hand," Shaker said, offering his.

Debbie took it. A second later, they were in her office. "Awesome," she said, turning to the demon. "Can you do this every morning and evening?"

"Yes," Shaker said, annoyed. "But sooner or later someone will observe us. I'd recommend teleporting only for special occasions. Besides, it takes a good deal of energy—"

"You teleport yourself everywhere, and come to my house to spend the night every evening," Debbie said pointedly. "I don't think it would take that much energy to stop and pick me up first."

Shaker rolled his eyes. "I'm feeling married. When am I going to get the perks as well as the responsibilities, Mistress?"

"When I forgive you for withholding info," Debbie said smoothly. "If Hell is so big on punishments, it should enjoy my punishing you. Be here at six."

Shaker growled in displeasure, then disappeared.

Sheila walked in. "Dante is here in the conference room. Giorgio is with him, unofficially representing you. Are you ready?"

Debbie nodded.

They walked down the hall to the large room. Dante was there with a lawyer and what looked like a bodyguard.

"In fear for your life?" Sheila sneered.

"She already killed my father," Dante said snidely. "I don't know she wouldn't try to kill me to stop me from revealing the truth."

"What bullshit are you selling now?" Debbie said. "I didn't kill Paul."

"I have a video that shows you giving Rebecca and Paul a bottle of wine," Dante said. "It shows my father drinking some, and then beginning to choke." He paused, expectant. "Can you guess what it shows next?"

Nothing, Shaker said in Debbie's mind. *Because demons do not show up on media. We appear as a blurry figure, or blackish smoke. He has nothing.*

"No," Debbie said triumphantly. "Why don't you tell me?"

The certainty in Dante's eyes flickered. "It shows my father writhing in pain, and you keeping Rebecca from helping him. Rebecca hits her head on a table, and goes down. Then it shows him missing and you running out of the room."

"Because that is exactly what happened," Debbie said confidently. "I told the police all of that. Paul was acting crazy. He struck Rebecca a glancing blow and she fell. While I was seeing to her, he ran out of the room. When I determined that Rebecca wasn't in danger, I went for help."

"Why didn't you call 911?" the lawyer asked. "There is a phone on your desk, Ms. Deal. Why leave the room at all?"

"Because I panicked," Debbie replied. "I also knew that there was at least one person at the party that knew CPR. Part of Rebecca's skull was crushed in. I wanted to get someone to help her. I was afraid she'd lose consciousness."

"But that isn't accepted First Aid procedure," the lawyer said. "The procedure is to call 911, then begin CPR."

Giorgio spoke up. "Listen, you two bit hack," he said politely. "Either charge her with something officially through the police, or get out of here. Ms. Deal is neither a licensed First Aid responder, nor is she a volunteer EMT. We have no requirement at Pandora for employees not designated as such to know any CPR procedures. Ms. Deal acted perfectly normal in a terrible situation."

"We have the tape," Dante said confidently. "That's evidence."

"It is evidence that what Debbie says happened really did happen. You have nothing, Dante, or you wouldn't be here talking to us, the police would." Giorgio stood up. "Unless you want to make an apology to Debbie, this meeting is over."

Dante glared at Debbie. "I'll get you before this is all over, you bitch." He stalked out, followed by his lawyer.

Giorgio turned to Debbie. "What I told him was all true. I don't think you have to worry about Dante charging you. He's got nothing. But I'm going to put you in touch with a friend of mine, Mr. Catarella. If Dante does actually file charges, he can represent you."

"Thanks, Giorgio," Debbie said gratefully. She and Sheila walked back to her office, closing the door after them.

"Well," Debbie said, sitting down in her chair. "Give me the status report. How is Pandora?"

"Flush with cash, hopefully, at 10am today," Sheila said happily. "Once we have that, we can resume filming on both *Absolution* and *Smoke and Ashes*. The furlough was good in one aspect: Jett Black is recovering very well, and is out of his cast. He should be able to do the rest of his own scenes with no needed stunt doubles."

"Good. How about *Hell's Gate*?"

"Ready to debut the last week of this month," Sheila said happily. "The new rating is all signed and sealed."

"Any new news?" Debbie prodded. "I know we don't have any cash yet to acquire more scripts, but are there any you were looking at?"

"Not yet, though the writer for *Smoke and Ashes* is hard at work on a sequel. And I do have some good actor news. The priest I hired for *Smoke and Ashes* is just wonderful. He had a few months of pastoral schooling before he left that behind to become an actor. He's a wealth of information." Sheila's tone became tentative. "I know that we have him dying at the end of *Smoke and Ashes* at the hands of one of the bad guys as another inspiration for the hero to keep fighting the good fight. But now I'm wondering if we shouldn't leave him badly wounded and unconscious in a hospital or something, so he could come back for the sequel."

Debbie considered various ideas, then snapped her fingers. "Or maybe as a ghost?"

Sheila's eyes got huge. "Or a demon! The second film could be all about his rise from the dead as a new enemy! We could call it *Out of the Ashes*."

"It is sheer gold," Debbie said, grinning widely. *What do you think, Shaker?*

I think it's possible, but improbable, came Shaker's mental reply. He sounded irritated. *Holy men of any faith are generally unrelenting in their beliefs, which makes them formidable enemies. They rarely change sides in death. Satan almost never makes them demons, unless you count the really bad ones, like Konrad Gröber.*

"Shaker's not buying it," Debbie said to Sheila grumpily.

"Harp's not either," Sheila said dourly. "Song suggests that we go with the ghost idea to have him come back to help the hero."

A demon partnering with a priest? Shaker said mentally to Debbie. *Never happens, except in B movies.*

"Everyone here or listening in mentally," Debbie said loudly. "A man who partners with a demon is our hero. This hero gets help from a defrocked priest who dies in movie one and comes back as a ghost in movie number two. Maybe he's barred from Hell and Heaven because of what he did. All of us listening know that sometimes the only way to win is to partner with others that might not be saints." Debbie paused. "Would that work?"

I think it's good, Shaker said approvingly. *Worth pursuing, at least. A demon-possessed man can't go certain places that the human or ghost could. Good plot twists.*

"Harp and Song approve," Sheila said. "And I do, too. I'll talk to the writer later today and tell her to write to that end."

Debbie smiled. "Anything else?"

Yes, Shaker intoned. *It's August, Mistress. About that favor—*

"No," Sheila said. "Other than I know it's your birthday tomorrow, and I wanted to take you to lunch today. I figured you'd taken the day off tomorrow."

Debbie sighed. She hadn't taken the day off, hadn't even planned anything special to do. *Forty-one years deserved some kind of celebration, didn't it?*

"See you at noon, Deb," Sheila said. "No arguments." She trotted out of the office.

I'll give you a choice in a week, Shaker. Will that be okay?

Yes, Shaker replied. *Call me when you're ready to go home. I'll be waiting.*

Debbie leaned back in her chair, staring off into space. How had this birthday crept up on her? What should she do to celebrate? Henry likely wouldn't be calling to offer up a last minute romantic dinner. He had never called again after that scene at her front door, not that she'd expected him to. His flowers had also stopped coming.

What would happen at the stock sale in December? Would Henry help her, or help Dante out of spite? Thank goodness she hadn't needed to sell Pandora Promos. Likely that deal had also disappeared.

The lunch with Sheila would have to be enough of a celebration. There was no time for anything else today. Reluctantly, Debbie pushed aside her worries and got back to work.

* * * *

"How much longer are they going to be?" Sheila said angrily, glaring at the young couple lingering over their drink remnants. "I want to sit at that table. That's where we sat for that first lunch, when you brought me here to thank me for my help on Pandora."

"I think they're going," Debbie said, waiting for the couple to get their coats on. Then, to her absolute outrage, they sat down again, the man fiddling with his phone.

"Son of a bitch," Sheila swore under her breath.

Debbie caught the sly glance of the woman as she looked over at them, then away, moving her straw around in her empty glass. Her fury escalated. *The woman at least is doing it deliberately, because she knows we're waiting for them to leave.*

The waiter brought the check, then the man signed it, still fiddling with his phone as he put on his suit jacket. The woman grabbed her purse, then the two of them sauntered past and out Andy's front door.

"Finally," Sheila said, plopping down at the table. "I thought they'd never leave."

Debbie took off her coat, but as she went to hang it on the back of the chair, she nearly bumped into the woman who'd just left. "Sorry," the woman said with a fake smile. "but did you see my phone? I think I left it here?"

She hadn't left anything. She was being obnoxious because her husband constantly ignored her. Debbie resisted the urge to speak, and glanced at the floor out of politeness. "Nothing's here. Sorry."

The woman didn't budge. "Can you look again?"

Her, Debbie thought venomously. *She's my choice, Shaker. And take the husband too for being an ass, as a birthday present from me.*

Of course, Mistress, Shaker replied immediately. *Thank you.*

"No," Debbie said evilly to the woman. "And I wouldn't waste any more of your life looking for a phone. Time's too precious, don't you think?"

The woman gave her an odd look, then left quickly. Debbie sank down into her chair.

"I should pick her for my next choice for Harp and Song," Sheila began thoughtfully. "She was a total bitch."

"Too late," Debbie said hastily. "I already called her for Shaker, and her hubby, too."

Sheila looked up, then made a face. "Dammit. Well, it's your birthday. Conceding that bitch and treating for lunch are the least I can do for my best friend." She smiled, then looked over the menu. "I definitely think we should be evil today, Deb. What do you think?"

"Oh yeah," Debbie said with a laugh.

* * * *

Debbie arranged for the following day off work right before she left, then called for Shaker. He arrived, whisking her home in a blink to a living room filled with flickering candles.

90

"What is this?" Debbie said, bewildered.

"You wanted something special," Shaker said gently. "I tried to create something with my limited means." He led her into the bathroom, where the Jacuzzi was frothing, steam rising up from its swirling water. Some wine lay ready with glasses on a platter, a familiar crest on the bottle. A plate of thick dark chocolates was piled high on a silver plate.

How had he paid for this? "You didn't have to."

"I wanted to, Mistress. Believe that if you believe nothing else." Shaker began undressing her carefully. "As for the how, the answer is simple: favors. The chocolates are from a friend in Switzerland. The wine is of the Triss vintage. And the candles are on loan from a coven in Massachusetts."

Debbie smiled, then stepped into the water, sinking into the warm depths. She turned to him. "Are you coming in?"

"Am I invited?" he asked.

"Yes," she replied.

Shaker removed his loincloth, and stepped carefully into the tub. He eased down next to her, then began massaging her shoulders, working down her body with his large hands to fondle and tease her flesh.

Debbie groaned, then went to move away.

Shaker stopped her. "Don't you want me anymore?" he whispered

Debbie closed her eyes, trying not to think of how much she wanted him. Before she could mask her feelings, Shaker felt her desire in her mind. His arms closed around her, bringing her tight against his body.

"Tell me you don't want this, any of it," he whispered huskily. "And I'll leave."

He's done terrible things.

He did them for you.

He's fucking wearing Amanda!

And who told him to take her as a victim? You did. It's not his fault he is what he is.

"Answer me," Shaker rumbled, moving against Debbie's naked skin. "I want to be within you, Mistress."

You're damned. Every month with him gets you deeper.

If I'm damned anyway. I might as well enjoy myself!

"Damnation is not all it's made out to be," Shaker whispered.

"You've given up and gone through so much, Mistress. Take what pleasure I can offer. Take what you know you deserve."

Debbie turned, the animalistic cry of passion loud in her ears as she clasped Shaker, pushing her lips to his. Her keening cry sharpened, climbing higher and higher as Shaker claimed her.

* * * *

Wake up, Mistress.

Debbie opened her eyes groggily. Instead of her cozy but compact bedroom, she was in a beautiful boudoir. Shaker was beside her, smiling slightly. "I thought maybe you'd sleep the day away."

Debbie sat up in bed, looking around. "Where are we?"

"A friend's home," Shaker supplied. He handed her a bathing suit. "Care for a swim before breakfast?"

Debbie smiled at the skimpy two-piece. "Are you wearing one?"

Shaker shook his head. "I'm going commando, as there is not a human about on this fine morning. And the others who are about won't care."

Debbie debated putting on the suit, then tossed it aside. "Then so will I. Lead on."

Shaker opened the large double doors across from the bed. The wind came through the opening in a sudden blast, stirring the curtains. "Come."

Debbie followed Shaker out onto a patio, the warm wind on her naked skin a blissfully unfamiliar experience. The sea was directly in front of them, the water cobalt blue. There was no one else on the long expanse of beach, except for seagulls crying on the wind. "Where are we?" she asked.

"A private island," Shaker said, offering his hand. "Come into the water. It's very warm."

Debbie took his hand, and together they waded into the water. It was indeed warm, the top surface shiny with reflected sunlight. But the depths were cool and refreshing; a little too cool for Debbie. She emerged with Shaker following, and walked up onto the white sand, stretching out on a sumptuous thick towel that lay spread out like a blanket. The heat baked into her body, erasing her slight chill and replacing it with a warm feeling of happiness.

"This is wonderful," Debbie said languidly. "Thank you for bringing me here."

"I wanted to do something special for you, Mistress." Shaker knelt down beside Debbie, and began to massage her feet.

Debbie sighed happily. "Is there a phone here? I should let Sheila know where I am in case there's some emergency—"

"I'll teleport you back tomorrow afternoon," Shaker interrupted firmly. "Sunday is early enough to think about your job. Now just relax and enjoy yourself, Mistress."

The peaceful lapping of the waves lulled Debbie just as much at Shaker's touch and the warm sunlight. Within moments, Debbie drifted into a deep relaxed sleep. When she awoke, her skin was pink with sunburn and the sun was low in the sky, the air cool enough to raise goosebumps on her skin. There was no sign of Shaker.

Debbie sat up in alarm. "Shaker?" Conscious of her nakedness, she wrapped herself in the towel and headed up to the house. That too, was empty. Debbie called repeatedly for Shaker but her cries—both mental and spoken—were unanswered. She opened the door to leave the house, ready to search the beach, and felt a sudden stabbing pain that brought her to her knees.

Chapter Eight

~ August ~

Debbie let out a scream, grabbing at her left side. *God, it felt like she was being stabbed!* Debbie curled up in a ball, tears leaking from her eyes.

The pain abruptly stopped. A gnawing hunger replaced it, ripping through her belly like a ravenous monster. Debbie scrambled to her feet, then hurried to the kitchen. She yanked open the refrigerator door and grabbed a jumbo packet of cold cuts. Tearing the plastic, she gobbled the entire package down as fast as she could. Tossing the plastic aside, she grabbed another, devouring that just as quickly. The writhing in her gut stopped, and she leaned against the counter, shaking slightly, worried that the pain would hit her again. But nothing happened.

Debbie carefully stood up straight, then inspected her left side. Her skin was unbroken. More amazing, it looked as if her sunburn was also going away.

Incredulous, Debbie went into the large full bath off the kitchen, and turned on the light, inspecting her naked body. Yes, her sunburn had faded and become a light tan. It was almost as if the meat had somehow helped her body to heal…

Mistress?

"Shaker!" Debbie yelled, her relief giving way to anger. "What the hell happened? Where are you?"

Shaker appeared before her. He was bloodied, his loin skin

spattered, and his torso coated with some kind of black inky mess. He gave her a cool look, then reached in back of her, grabbing a large towel. "That couple you sent me for?" he said curtly. "The man not only had a gun, but actually knew how to use it."

"You were shot?"

"Several times at point blank range," he replied, wetting the cloth and wiping at the blackness on his skin. He got most of it off, then tossed the towel in the garbage. He turned on the shower, then removed his loincloth, also placing that in the trash.

Guess he'd be making a new loincloth very soon. But out of who? "Are you okay? I felt you get hit—"

"—and you did the right thing, to eat meat," Shaker finished, stepping into the shower. "You can join me if you want to, Mistress."

Not going to happen. "I'll wait out here, thanks."

"As you wish."

Shaker took so long showering that Debbie left for the bedroom. She looked in the closets and dressers, finding some yoga pants, a sports bra, and a sweatshirt that fit her decently. Dressed, she went in search of wine. When Shaker emerged clean an hour later, she was sitting on the balcony, sipping her drink as she looked out over the sea.

Shaker wrapped himself in a robe, and sat down beside her. "I don't feel any pain in you now, Mistress. But that doesn't mean you're all right."

"I was scared to death," Debbie said softly. "I thought I was dying." She poured a bit more wine into her glass.

Shaker got up, went inside, and brought out a glass for himself. Pouring some wine into it, he took a small swallow. "You can't die of a wound I sustain, unless I die myself. Even then, death is not a certainty."

Debbie looked over at him. "But you said I could die. The pain was terrible. What if I have a heart attack from the shock next time you get hurt?"

"That can happen, but with your youth and health it's unlikely," Shaker replied. "The pain you feel is through a mental link, not in your body. When it happens again, do what you did, and seek out flesh. It will help to not only heal me through our mental link, but also alleviate your symptoms."

"Like it alleviated my sunburn?" Debbie commented wryly.

"You have some other benefits of being demon bound, besides the obvious ones," Shaker said with a smile. "Flesh will not heal a grievous wound you sustain, not with our relationship so young. But slight problems like sunburn or the common cold can be easily alleviated with a little raw meat—"

"It wasn't raw meat," Debbie corrected, chuckling. "It was cold cuts. I ate two packages."

"Those were raw sirloin strips for stir frying," Shaker said, raising his eyebrows. "Though I'm sure that in your condition they tasted as good as any cooked meat you'd ever had."

Debbie set down her glass fast, wine slopping over the rim to spatter on the table. She swallowed hard, her gorge rising.

Shaker got out of his chair and went to her, hugging her. "Shh," he soothed gently. "Don't think about it, Mistress. It's not important. What is important is we're both alive and unscathed."

"I can't do this," Debbie whispered. "I can't do this, Shaker."

"You've already done it," Shaker encouraged. "The hard part is over."

Debbie clutched him and didn't answer, her eyes on the unrelenting blackness of the dark horizon.

* * * *

Debbie awoke the next morning in her same clothes. Shaker was beside her, reading a book. With surprise, she recognized it as a recently published popular fiction novel.

Shaker caught her look, folded down the page, and put the book aside. "We demons can't always be reading erotica," he said with a laugh. "Not that I'd oppose a little morning delight, if you're in the mood."

Oddly, Debbie was very in the mood as she looked at Shaker's muscular torso. But she pushed her desires down. "What do we have, Shaker?"

Shaker tilted his head quizzically. "You mean our relationship, I take it?"

"Yes."

"What do you want it to be?"

"Damn it!" Debbie yelled angrily, losing her composure. "Don't answer me with a question! Tell me what you want from me!"

"What you're willing to give," Shaker replied easily.

"No! That's not good enough! I want to know what you really want out of our arrangement!"

The casual expression Shaker always wore cracked. For a moment, despair and anger showed through. "What do you want me to say?" he rumbled in a low voice. "You want me to be romantic and say I want your love, that I love you? You want me to tell me you're free to fuck whomever you want and I'll still come to your bed on the nights you'll have me?"

Debbie did not back down. "I want the truth, you asshole!"

"Fine," Shaker said bitterly. He stood and faced her. "The truth is that I don't expect anything: not your kindness, not your love, not your sex, not your loyalty and not your monogamy." His eyes were red and furious. "I have had many Mistresses in my life, and they've run the gamut from evil sadist to chaste temptress, Debbie. I don't expect to be treated fairly anymore."

Debbie snorted. "You expect me to feel sorry for you? You murder people and make clothes out of their skin! You eat them!"

"I am a demon, and that is what demons do!" Shaker shouted, his booming tone rattling the windows in their frames.

"Which means that you don't feel badly about any of what you've done," Debbie continued stridently. "You are not human, yet you expect me to treat you like one, to feel sorry for your plight!"

"I don't feel badly about what I've done, or what I'll do," Shaker retorted. "I don't expect you to treat me like your boyfriend, or even a friend." His tone had changed from angry to resigned. "But I do have feelings, even if they aren't the same depth as yours are."

Debbie gaped at him, surprised.

"I'm not a romantic hero, nor am I a cardboard one-dimensional villain whose only impulse is to do evil," Shaker explained. "Those are the two popular human perceptions, and both are wrong."

"Then what are you?" Debbie said sarcastically. "My savior?"

"I'm a slave," Shaker said sadly. "And this is all there is for me." He turned and left. Debbie called for him after a moment, but he didn't reply.

* * * *

That afternoon, Shaker returned Debbie to her house, then abruptly left again.

Debbie fixed herself some dinner, then watched some mindless TV. After replaying a scene four times and still not comprehending the joke being told, she switched it off and thought about what Shaker had said.

When I really examine the rules of our arrangement, Shaker is a slave.

Debbie wasn't sure how to feel about that. On one hand, she felt bad about his lack of choices. On the other, she had paid quite a bit in pain and deeds for his services. Their arrangement had been at his suggestion. And no matter how guilty the truth of the matter rendered her, it was simply very gratifying to come home to a being whose duty it was to please you and take your mind off your troubles.

There was only one question to answer, really: what she wanted for herself. Shaker had said he wouldn't stand in the way if Debbie wanted a relationship with someone else. Maybe things hadn't worked out well with Henry, but that didn't mean she couldn't date others. The question was did she want to?

Debbie went to her bedroom, changed from her work clothes to her pajamas, and slipped beneath the covers. She lay awake, staring at the ceiling and pondering her options.

I really don't want to date anyone.

Henry's demands had been too much. Maybe she didn't get flowers anymore, but Shaker supplied everything else, including mind-blowing sex. Guiltily, Debbie conceded that her contentment with the current arrangement lay in her role of Mistress. The normal pressure to be a lover, wife, mother, or hostess was absent, and Debbie wasn't eager to feel it anytime soon. She was too busy with Pandora.

* * * *

The next two weeks passed uneventfully, the uneasy silence between her and Shaker continuing. Debbie wasn't sure where he was spending his nights, but it wasn't with her. He spent as little time in her company as possible, ferrying her to and from work, and then disappearing.

Debbie was uncomfortable with the situation, but not sure how to resolve it. She also had her hands full.

Dante had dropped the lawsuit, but he still found ways to cause trouble, usually through Titan. Henry hadn't shown up with him again, but other Titan reps had, accusing Debbie of everything from stealing movie ideas to faking company revenues. So far, Giorgio and his new protégé Mr. Catarella had been able to fend off all the potential lawsuits, but they were exhausted. Debbie was also behind in her own work from the countless planning sessions she'd had to attend and the statements she'd had to give to make the lawsuits go away.

Debbie told herself to focus on the good and not the bad. Pandora was flush with money again due to Mrs. Triss, and Sheila had been hard at work with Acquisitions, working on that sequel to *Smoke and Ashes.* They'd signed all the original actors, and shooting had begun last week. *Hell's Gate* had been released to critics, and the first review to come back had been five-star. The man had raved about the film; so what if he wasn't with Newsweek or The Times? Sheila also was in negotiations for another three promising productions, each of which Debbie was pleased to see did not have any demons in the major roles. Sheila, to Debbie's surprise, was concerned about that.

"We've made our success this year with supernatural films," Sheila had mentioned at their last spa visit, as their nails were drying. "I'm worried about moving away from that, Deb. We might want to do one picture with no paranormal slant, but the other new pieces should have some supernatural aspect, even if it's not demon."

"Like what?" Debbie had scoffed. "Vampires? They've been done to death."

"Maybe some new kind of monster," Sheila mused, looking at her new polish. "Maybe something with talons."

"Werecats?" Debbie chuckled. "Or were you thinking wereeagles?"

Sheila stuck out her tongue at Debbie. "I just wanted to mention it. Pandora's been very successful with our current genres. I don't want to jeopardize that."

The idea of some kind of strange new monster struck a chord in Debbie. She had spent that night at home on her laptop, looking up animals and trying to determine if they'd be believable as a new creation. No matter how interesting she thought the idea, the public had to buy into it, or it wasn't worth making the movie. But try as she might, nothing came to mind that night, or any other night since then.

Her phone beeping snapped Debbie back into the present. She pressed the intercom button. "Yes?"

"There is a Mr. Cahill to see you."

Debbie picked up the phone. "Does he have an appointment?"

"No," her new secretary whispered. "But I recognize him as that actor from *Smoke and Ashes*. He looks pretty serious."

Shit, even if his reason for seeing her was a complete waste of her time, she had to see him or risk influencing the sequel. "Show him in."

Debbie rose from her desk, ready to shake the man's hand. The door opened and a fiftyish man walked in, his white hair neatly styled, his clothes a casual shirt and jeans.

"Hello, Mr. Cahill," Debbie said, taking a step. "I—"

Run! Shaker bellowed in her mind. *He's here to kill you!*

Debbie froze, then stumbled backward, the thrust of the serrated knife missing her by inches as Cahill lunged at her. She got the desk between them, and then Shaker appeared, his howl of pain screeching as the knife sunk deep into his left forearm. Instantly, Debbie felt a twinge of pain in her left arm.

"Holy Mary, Mother of God, pray for me!" Cahill bellowed. "Christ, son of God, pray for me!"

Debbie backed up until she hit the wall, terrified. *He's a real priest. One of those true believers Shaker talked about!*

Shaker screeched again, grabbing for the man. Cahill evaded him, slicing open another long gash. Song appeared behind Cahill, blocking the door. Harp appeared a second later, scooting over between Debbie and the still circling fighters.

Debbie watched anxiously from behind Harp, sure Shaker would bring this to a fast end. He was twice the size of Cahill, and much more muscular. But to her horror, Shaker seemed unable to touch the priest. Cahill kept up a constant chant of prayer as he attacked, his knife sliding deep again and again. With every new wound, her own pain grew worse and worse until her body was throbbing with agony. Debbie pushed it away, yet her panic rose notch by notch, until she was panting with fear. *Why wasn't Shaker killing him?*

"Do something," Harp said angrily, turning to Debbie. "Kill the priest!"

Debbie recoiled. "Why can't you?"

"He's protected by his faith," the demon said with a snarl. "We can't even touch him. You don't do it and Shaker's going to lose. And you're going to die."

Debbie cast around her, looking for a weapon. The closest thing she saw was the group of pens on her desk. If she tried to stab Cahill with one of those, she'd get knifed for sure...*I need a weapon!*

Desk bottom drawer, at the back, Shaker replied in Debbie's mind. *Push the red button, grip it with both hands, point and fire. Do it now, or we're finished!*

Debbie scrambled for the drawer, shoving papers out of the way. Her hand hit cold metal. She lifted out a semi auto .44 equipped with a silencer, then almost dropped it as fresh pain lanced through her

Shoot him, Mistress!

Debbie took aim under Harp's arm, pointed, and shot. The bullet went wild. But it did get Cahill's attention. He lunged for her.

Shoot him!

Debbie yanked the trigger. The gun fired, the bullet striking Cahill in the throat. He was knocked off his feet, falling backward to the floor.

Again! Finish him!

Debbie stepped closer to the writhing priest, and shot him several more times. Cahill stopped moving at the second shot, but she was taking no chances.

"He's gone," Shaker said, sinking to his knees.

Debbie set the gun carefully on her desk, then looked at the man lying in a pool of blood. Everything was surreal, like a movie. "This is going to ruin the sequel," she said finally.

"And your carpet," Song added. "You'd do better to get laminate in here, Debbie."

"Make the secretary forget she saw him come in here," Shaker said to Song. She hurried out. He turned to the other remaining demon. "Harp, tell Sheila what happened. Tell her to arrange a shooting scene today, and have you stand in. Stage an accident."

"Stand in?" Debbie repeated.

"We can't touch them while their soul is still inside," Harp said evilly. "But when it's gone, so is their faith barrier." He stepped into the body, his physical form dissolving into black smoke that seeped through the priest's clothes and skin. The priest sat up, giving Debbie a wide grin. He stood, then buttoned up his jacket, covering the bloodstains and bullet holes in his shirt. "I can't do anything about the back, Shaker," Harp said in the priest's voice. He turned, trying to peer over his shoulder. "How's it look?"

"Like you got shot," Shaker replied. "Go to his trailer and change…wait, it's probably filled with bibles and holy stuff. Try another trailer on the lot. Sheila can point you in the right direction."

Sheila ran in, hurrying to Debbie and hugging her. "Are you okay?"

"We'll be okay," Harp said out of Carhill's mouth, "if you get me a new shirt and arrange a shooting scene today so I can die publicly."

"Come on," Sheila said, taking his hand. "I'll escort you. If anyone asks, we'll say its stage blood, that you accidentally popped the fake blood bags ahead of schedule, so we need to reshoot the scene. We'll go to Mick's trailer."

They disappeared. Song came back in, looking pleased. "The secretary has been handled. But there will be a little matter of some favors owed for this, Shaker…"

"We're even from now on," Shaker said with reluctance. "Help Harp with whatever he needs. I can make it from here on my own."

Song nodded and disappeared.

Debbie had recovered by that time enough to make her way to Shaker and look him over. His wounds weren't healing, but the bleeding seemed to have stopped.

"Are you okay?"

"No," Shaker said weakly. "That was a blessed knife. These wounds will scar. But I won't die from them, if that's what you're asking." He stood. "I may have to stay with you for tonight, Mistress—"

Debbie clasped his hand. "Take us home."

* * * *

"You didn't have to cook for me," Shaker said hesitantly from his prone position on the couch.

"I didn't," Debbie said, bringing him another plate of raw beef. "This is just warmed up so it's not frozen solid."

"I was trying to bring in some levity, but thank you," Shaker said, sitting up. He devoured the meat, then handed back the plate. Lying down, he again covered himself with a blanket. Debbie took the plate into the kitchen, then fixed herself a sandwich.

Shaker had saved her life. The priest had come to kill her. He would have, if Shaker hadn't been keeping watch. He'd been a real priest, not a used-to-be one. How had he found out about her and Shaker?

"If you come in here," Shaker called out. "We can discuss your questions."

Debbie went into the living room, and sat on the couch next to Shaker. "How did he find us?"

"Remember that man you met at the festival?" Shaker said. "Devlin? He's more than a man, so his sense of smell is far more acute. He could smell which of you humans was bound to me. The priest may have done the same thing... It just took him longer."

"What would he smell? Fire and brimstone?"

"A faint scent of sulfur, possibly. But more likely something stinky like hot tar or burning plastic. To men of faith, evil smells noxious, literally. So it would be something noticeably nasty."

"Why did he come after me?"

"To send me back to Hell," Shaker said, clasping her hand in his. "The easiest way to send a demon back to Hell is to kill their master. He planned to kill you."

"In my office on a weekday?" Debbie sputtered, incredulous. "My secretary was right outside!"

"Men of faith rarely concern themselves with the laws of the world," Shaker said darkly. "Their leader often takes care of them quite well in that regard."

"What do you mean?"

"That you'd have been murdered and no one would have admitted to seeing the man," Shaker said. "Likely your secretary would have forgotten him as soon as he walked out your door, your blood dripping from his hands."

"So those on Heaven's side have some righteous cloak of invisibility?"

"If they are destroying my kind, yes," Shaker said darkly. "But I don't have any profound truths to tell you about the battle of good and evil, Mistress. I'm just a foot soldier who follows orders."

Debbie rubbed her eyes. "It's going to be Hell finding a replacement for him."

"Not at all," Shaker soothed. "You'll think of something clever, you and Sheila. You always do."

"We'll work it into the script," Debbie said. She patted Shaker on the arm, then yanked her hand back with a grimace. "Sorry! Did that hurt?"

"Not as much as you sending me away," Shaker said, sitting up and grabbing her hand in his.

"Let me go," Debbie said, trying to pull her hand back.

"Not until you tell me why you sent me away," he persisted.

"I don't want to talk about it now," Debbie said firmly. "Goodnight, Shaker."

Shaker let her go. He laid back, his red eyes unfathomable. "Goodnight, Mistress."

Chapter Nine

~ September ~

Debbie stood at her office window staring out at the street far below, contemplating jumping.

Just as Pandora had seemed to be coming out of the red permanently, disaster had struck.

Hell's Gate first review had been 5-star. But that was the only five-star rating it had gotten. Most of the reviews had been average at best, with some substantially lower. That hadn't been so bad. Debbie could live with bad reviews so long as the ticket sales were good. But the sales had been mediocre, at best. Several moral groups had denounced the movie publicly. Usually that would have brought the kids streaming into the theaters, but the groups had brought enough pressure on the theater owners to cause them not to admit anyone under 17 unless an adult was present. Some theaters had pulled the movie altogether. Those two things combined had cut the expected proceeds in half. Sheila was upbeat, saying with a little marketing that DVD sales would make back twice over what they were losing now. But that didn't help Pandora's current quarter.

The priest Cahill's "accident" on the set had drawn a lot of good publicity. The writer had written his death into the script as previously planned, with Cahill coming back as a ghost. But with this second death linked to Pandora, the police had come by and begun to interview everyone, asking a lot of questions. Both Debbie and Sheila had answered their questions, but it had hurt production of the sequel to *Smoke and Ashes*. The police didn't want to believe that a clip of blanks had caused the death of Cahill. They had the body now and were doing an autopsy. Shaker assured her that Harp had taken out the bullets—just *how* he'd done so wasn't specified—so there would be nothing for the coroner to find. Debbie had been waiting all this morning for a call telling her the charade was over, that they'd found a piece of real bullet in the corpse.

Titan was coming again this afternoon with another lawsuit. Dante would almost certainly be there...Debbie thought again about opening the window and jumping. One quick act and it would be over...

Mistress? Shaker said in her mind. *Don't lose hope. We've had some setbacks, but we're in a good position. In fact, I have another investor who would like to meet with you tonight. Say seven-thirty?*

"Sure," Debbie said aloud. Her phone began to ring. Startled, she hurried to the desk and answered it, whispering a prayer for no real bullet pieces.

"Mrs. Dead?"

Debbie blanched. "This is Ms. Deal. Hello?"

"Oh, sorry. The last letter on the file looked like a 'd.' My name is Detective O'Hara. I believe I talked with your VP, Sheila?"

Get to the point already! "Do you have any news, detective?"

"Nothing you're not already aware of," O'Hara said casually, then paused.

Debbie waited in silence, resisting the urge to say anything, knowing it was what the officer wanted.

"There were no bullets in the body," O'Hara said finally. "But there are entry wounds like several bullets hit Cahill. No signs of anything being removed. The coroner said it was as though they hit him and disappeared."

"Bizarre," Debbie said.

"Very," O'Hara agreed. "All we can surmise is that the blanks were packed wrong, and somehow some of them did have something organic that struck the victim and caused his death. This is going to be ruled an accident."

Debbie grasped the desk edge in relief, sinking down into her chair.

"Good."

There was silence from the phone, then O'Hara began speaking his tone cold. "This is the third death associated with your company, Ms. Deal, since you took the helm. Counting your former partner, that makes four—"

"I can't help that some people have mental problems, or that they snap under stress," Debbie said evenly. "Film is a high stress business, Mr. O'Hara."

"—two suicides, one accident, one murder, and let's not forget the two disappearances, either. I'd say it was a bad thing to cross you, Ms. Deal."

"On the contrary," Debbie said icily. "Losing Mr. Cahill has been a disaster, as was losing Rebecca. She was a dear friend. The disappearances were also terrible blows, as both employees were personal acquaintances of mine, and hard to replace."

"I won't take up any more of your time," O'Hara said. "But I will be in touch, Ms. Deal."

Debbie hung up the phone. Then she grabbed her jacket and purse, heading for the door. She needed to see Sheila.

* * * *

"You've got to go on, Father," the little girl pleaded. "You can't give up now."

The young man by her side shot the evil ringleader in the forehead, then turned back to his dying friend and mentor, resignation creasing his worn face.

"Father?" the little girl said again hopefully.

The man in her arms was riddled with bullets, his face a dead ringer for Cahill. His eyes fluttered. "At least...we saved you, Lindsay."

"Fight, damn you," the young man said angrily. "Don't die on us! Not when we won!"

"Storm...you take care of her...promise?"

"Of course," the young man called Storm said gruffly. He turned, but not before a tear traced down his dusty cheek.

"You be a good girl...Lindsay," the dying priest said. He touched her cheek gently with his hand. "Be good."

107

"I will," the little girl bawled, clutching him tighter. "I love you, Father."

The priest sagged, his arm falling away from Lindsay's cheek. She began to howl.

"CUT!" the director yelled. "That's it, we got it!"

Lindsay wiped at her tears, then climbed to her feet, the priest beside her sitting up to take Storm's offered hand.

"We're done for the day, people," the director called. "Great job everyone! Be here tomorrow at 5 a.m., ready to go. We still need that sunrise scene."

There was a round of sighs as people gathered their things and went to their trailers.

"Excellent," Sheila said with approval. She shook the director's hand.

"Your finding Garwood to replace Cahill is what was excellent," he answered. "We've got all the scenes done now, except the one with the sunrise. Hopefully we'll get that tomorrow, and then we can focus on editing."

Debbie walked up, flashing a smile. "That was wonderful! Brought a mist to my eyes for sure." *And Jett Black was looking more than the picture of health as the hero, Storm. Damn, was he sexy...*

"We'll knock them dead," the director said with a laugh. Then his face went white, and he mumbled an excuse as he ran to talk to the cameraman.

"Everyone's a little spooked since Cahill's death," Sheila whispered to Debbie. "The staff thinks the picture is cursed."

"It seems to be," Debbie said darkly. "Unless it's just us. But that scene was really great. *Smoke and Ashes* is going to be a hit." She paused. "Are you available tonight? Shaker set up a meeting with another investor."

Sheila shook her head. "I have to catch a flight to that meeting in Denver about that river picture." She grimaced. "I'd teleport, but Harp and Song say their already overdue for a feeding, and I haven't had time to choose—"

"That's okay," Debbie said hastily. "I can do it myself. I just wanted to invite you if you were here."

"Who is the investor?" Sheila asked. "Another human with demon connections?"

Debbie shook her head. "I don't know. But if I were to guess, I'd say yes."

"Hmm," Sheila said, narrowing her eyes. "I'll reschedule that flight. I want to be here for this one."

* * * *

At seven-thirty, Debbie got up from her chair and went for the third time to the window.

Patience, Mistress, Shaker said in her mind. *The man coming has much that occupies his nights. I have it on good authority that he will be here as soon as he can.*

Sheila's pen began to beat a staccato on the wooden top of the conference table. "I'm starving," she said irritably. "Maybe we should order in something? Harp could bring up a pizza."

"I'm not hungry," Debbie said absently, scanning the streets below. The rain was thick, pounding the pavement. The curb was bare all the way up the block.

He will not come that way, Mistress. In fact, he is already at your threshold.

There was a knock at Debbie's office door. Before she could yell come in, the door opened and in walked the tall blonde man from the festival. He was followed by the man in black, who looked as foul-tempered as he had the last time.

The blonde man strode up.

Devlin, Shaker said in Debbie's mind. *Offer your hand.*

"Thank you for coming, Devlin," Debbie said pleasantly, extending her hand. Devlin smiled and took it. Instead of shaking it, he kissed the back of it gently. Then he did the same to Sheila.

"Good to see you both again," he said, each word like a deft caress. "I hear you are in need of financing. Hopefully, we can come to terms for our mutual benefaction." He gestured to the table. "Please sit."

Sheila and Debbie glanced at one another quickly at his assuming control, then sat.

"You have done a great deal for demonkind with your movies,"

Devlin said. "I'm willing to fund your company in quite a substantial way if you'll consent to doing the same for my kind."

Shaker said he was more than man. "What did you have in mind?" Debbie said.

"What kind?" Sheila said more bluntly.

Vampire-kind, Shaker said mentally.

Devlin bared his teeth, revealing upper and lower fangs. "The vampires, my dear Sheila."

His sharp teeth might have scared Debbie a year ago. But after all she'd been through in the past few months, a real vampire didn't even phase her. "Let me say again, what did you have in mind, Devlin?"

"A movie, or maybe a movie series," Devlin said thoughtfully. "Featuring vampires as the good guys."

"You're about a decade too late," Sheila said derisively. "Those have been done to death. Zombies, too."

"You misunderstand me," Devlin said more forcefully. "I do not want a movie made for teens. I want a series of movies made for adults, something with a little romance—"

"With all due respect, Devlin," Debbie said apologetically. "We can't agree to make a movie, much less a series, that we know won't bring in a return on your investment. Sheila is right in that there is a glut of movies right now with vampires and zombies. We need a new monster."

"How about a weresnake?" the man in black said gruffly. "You don't ever hear about them in film."

Debbie pursed her lips, trying fast for a good reply that wouldn't provoke him. "Maybe as a villain," she said finally. "Snakes have a lot of connections to evil—"

"We do not," the man in black said angrily. His voice had a hissing tone. Debbie's eyes widened as his shifted slightly the round pupils narrowing to vertical slits.

"Stop that, Lash," Devlin ordered. "We are never going to get anywhere with threats."

Lash muttered something under his breath, his pupils resuming their human shape.

"You may have something," Sheila said slowly. "He's right that

110

snakes haven't been done very much in supernatural films. And this year is the Chinese Year of the Snake. We may be able to add in a weresnake as a bit player to the sequel to *Smoke and Ashes*." She looked at Lash. "I can't promise that he'd be a good guy though."

"So long as you don't make him a candy ass," Lash hissed, then smiled.

"Back to my proposal," Devlin interrupted. "If you could not do a series, could you maybe insert a vampire into one of your other series, instead?"

"That's doable," Debbie said, nodding. "We were looking at a historical piece set in Europe, but we don't have any particular details worked out yet. Not even a title."

"What is the plot?" Devlin asked.

"The usual," Sheila said with a smile. "Guy finds girl, guy loves girl, guy loses girl, then guy roams the world through the ages looking to avenge her and right the wrongs of an apocalyptic world."

"Hmm," Devlin said, "I could work with that most definitely, but I would require a little adjustment to be made." He beamed at them. "And complete control over the film."

"We don't do that," Debbie said flatly. "Ever."

"Why not?" Devlin asked. "I'm happy to finance the film completely. And I'll give you enough cash to infuse Pandora with enough life to keep going even if all your movies flop in the coming year. What do you have to lose?"

"Our reputation," Sheila replied. "I'm being blunt with you here to save you making a mistake; vampire movies for adults don't do well. Teens and preteens are the ones with the disposable cash. Even aiming for college kids is risky anymore."

"This one will," Devlin said with surety. "It will be different."

Debbie groaned inwardly. *Everyone coming into film always said their stuff was different. But Devlin was right that Pandora had a lot to gain by taking his deal. Devlin could find out his own way that his product had no market. If his movie was the only one that flopped, Pandora's reputation wouldn't suffer.*

"I can accept your deal," Debbie said to Devlin. "Provided you give me a contract in writing stipulating the amount that you will give us for financing, and a clause promising that the amount pledged will not change no matter how the movie we make for you does in sales. We also need you to specify that the movie you will oversee personally will be financed completely by you, and that you will be responsible for all costs, including marketing, distribution, and production, for which we will provide work resources at the going price at the time of filming."

"I agree to your terms," Devlin said with a nod. "I'll have my attorney draw up the papers for you." He stood up and offered his hand. "I think we have a deal, Ms. Deal."

"That's it?" Lash grumbled as he stood. "What about my idea?"

"Let me look into some of the new pictures," Sheila responded. "I think that we could definitely do something with a weresnake in one of them."

"Adieu," said Devlin, then he headed for the door.

Lash shot Sheila a grin, then followed Devlin outside, shutting the door after them.

They have gone, Shaker said in Debbie's mind, his tone pleased. *Well done, Mistress.*

"You know he's not going to want to pay us any more money after that picture of his flops," Sheila said tiredly.

"He'll be under contract," Debbie replied. "He won't have a choice."

"Forgive me, but he didn't seem like the most likely person to do anything he didn't want to," Sheila griped. "Sorry, I should say 'most likely vampire'. And that man with him was some kind of snakeman or something!"

"Do not be so sure that the picture will flop," Shaker said, materializing with Song and Harp. "Devlin can be very charismatic when he wants to be. I can believe any tale of his would be equally enthralling, at least to women."

"Either way, it's good for Pandora," Debbie said. She turned to Sheila. "Did you mean it about that weresnake role? I'm thinking that Mr. Lash is going to be asking about it the next time he comes here with his boss."

"Actually, yes," Sheila said thoughtfully. "I never considered a snake. It's very original. But the problem is making the role a hero. I just don't think we're going to get people to embrace a snake as something good."

"Maybe not here in America," Debbie said. "But in the Asian countries, we might have a very good chance. Check into it. Run some numbers."

Sheila nodded. "Will do." She paused. "By the way, I really like your new 'do. I think you were born to be a blonde."

Debbie flushed slightly, shaking her head so the new layers fluffed around her face. "Thanks. It feels a lot better shorter."

"Are you ready to go home, Mistress?" Shaker asked.

"Yes," Debbie replied, picking up her coat. "I'll see you tomorrow, Sheila."

"Goodnight," Sheila said, taking Harp's hand as he materialized beside her.

Debbie and Shaker arrived home in a blink.

"I'll be in the guest bedroom," Shaker said. "Call if you need anything." He left the room, shutting the bedroom door behind him.

Debbie put away her coat and purse, then went to her own bedroom. She slipped out of her work clothes and showered, then put on her flannel nightgown. The nights were already chilly, and she wouldn't be having the benefit of demon heat in her bed tonight.

Shaker hadn't made any sexual advances to Debbie since he'd been injured by the priest. His wounds had scarred, and were healing slowly. While Debbie was slightly frustrated after close to a month, she didn't want to push Shaker for sex. His labeling himself a slave still bothered her. The least she could do for now was not treat him like one.

Chapter Ten

~ October ~

Demons ran down the sidewalk, chasing one another. A boy dressed in a metallic cloth cowboy suit and wraparound sunglasses pointed his six-shooter at them, yelling for them to wait up. Debbie smiled, looking out through her house window.

"I told you optioning costumes for Halloween could be lucrative," Sheila said happily from behind her. "We've sold ten thousand units at last count."

"You are my number one gal," Debbie said with a crazy leer, then laughed maniacally, emulating the Joker.

Sheila gave her a look. "You need to quote Ledger, not Nicholson, or no one is going to get your movie quotes, Ms. Joker, even with your green hair."

"Sorry," Debbie giggled, applying the last of the white face paint to her cheeks. "I'm just having fun. I haven't dressed up for ages. This costume party was a great idea."

"Not mine, unfortunately," Sheila said, smoothing down her black wig. "While I like playing dress up, I am not looking forward to seeing anyone from Titan Pictures. But I do understand we need to make an appearance. The great news is that our demons can come as they are." She turned to Debbie, her heavily shadowed eyes gleaming in her chalk white face. "You might run into Henry. Are you ready for that?"

"You might run into Devlin," Debbie quipped. "Are you ready to be a real vampire's bride?"

Sheila grabbed Debbie's arm. "Deb, I'm serious about Henry. You told me how he came on so strong and then just never called you again. That was weird! To have sent you all those flowers for months and that spa package, then to just stop all communication because you won't sleep with him—"

"He's a top level executive," Debbie said flatly. "I'm sure he didn't miss the money. And his behavior just shows he was after one thing."

"I just don't want you to get hurt."

Debbie bit her lip, smearing a little of her red lipstick on her teeth. "I'm over him, Sheila. If I see him, I'll be polite. But that's all."

Sheila took a tissue, chuckling. "You're the vampire now. Hold still." She wiped the red lipstick off Debbie's teeth. "Come on, or we'll be late."

The two women walked out of the bathroom into the living room, where the three demons waited. Shaker looked as he always did, though his loincloth was freshly made. Harp and Song were dressed in black togas, the former carrying a harp made of grey bones that looked to be real. Debbie almost asked if it was, then thought better of it.

"You both look lovely," Shaker said, offering his hand to Debbie. "Shall we?"

The fivesome teleported, ending up just outside the gates to a large conference center. They walked through the open gates down a well-lit paved path to a door, where the doorman was checking in guests. Debbie gave her name and Sheila's, and the doorman checked them off his list. The group entered, walking into a large room bedecked with orange and black crepe, spiders, bats, and all other manner of Halloween trappings.

"The decorator must have charged a fortune," Sheila said appraisingly. "This is just gorgeous."

"Most everything, anyway," Debbie commented irritably. "There's Dante."

Her nemesis was standing at a table, a fairy model on one arm, talking to a few men in Roman costumes. He was dressed as a demon, complete with red skin, black horns, and shiny black leather pants.

"Aptly dressed," Sheila noted, taking a glass of champagne from a passing waiter.

"I think I'm offended," Shaker said mockingly. "That child has only the conception of petty evil."

"He's evil enough to annoy me," Debbie said. She turned to Shaker. "If you can ever find a way, you know…he'd be my first choice."

"I'm working on it," Shaker said irritably, then moved away in the crowd.

"What's with him?" Sheila asked Debbie.

"He doesn't like being compared to humans," Song explained. "He thinks your race is insignificant next to ours."

Debbie was not going to get into another long conversation of demon versus human, especially when she wasn't sure that the views Shaker presented to others was what he really thought at all. "I'm going to head over and get some food," she said to Sheila. "Want some?"

"Not yet," Sheila said, patting her hair. "As soon as I eat, I have to give up my hopes of looking stunning in this dress."

"I told you, Dev will not be here, Mistress," Song murmured. "He has other business this Hallow's Eve."

Debbie smiled as she walked away. *Who knew vampires could make such an impression without a single kiss, much less a bite on the neck?* But she did have to admit Dev was sexy.

"Ms. Deal," a voice said from behind her. "How good to see you."

Debbie turned. A young woman stood there, her tiara shining brightly, her full length wedding dress an ivory satin with many crystals and pearls all over the bodice. Her brown hair was pinned up, just a few curls escaping the bun. There was something familiar about her.

"Hello," Debbie said pleasantly, her mind working overtime to come up with a name.

"Mrs. Triss," the woman said pleasantly, extending her left hand. The diamond ring on it was large…and also familiar.

Had she magically grown young? Triss had mentioned those potions given to her by the demon. "Hello," Debbie managed. "You must be the daughter your mother spoke of at our lunch. It's good to meet you."

"Yes," the young Mrs. Triss replied. "I regret to say my mother had a bad stroke last week. She passed away soon after."

"I'm sorry to hear that," Debbie said. "She seemed like a very nice woman." *This might mean that the Triss-Pandora partnership was over.*

116

Thank goodness she'd found Devlin.

"She wasn't," the girl said, then smiled. "But she could be kind to those she liked. And I know she liked you, from the little she told me about you. I hope we can be friends, as you were with her."

Here's the opening to find out where Pandora stands now. "I'd like that," Debbie said cordially. "Do you share her interest in movies?"

"No," Mrs. Triss said with a smile. "But I do share Rack's interest in your studio."

Debbie stared at the girl, realizing at once what had happened. *The mother had died. And her human child by her late husband, likely groomed since birth for the relationship, had taken over her mother's position in every way...including marrying the demon.*

"I'm still a novice at investing," Mrs. Triss admitted. "But Rack knows good investments, or so Mama always said. The money will continue to funnel into Pandora. I just wanted to make you aware of the change."

"Yes," Debbie said, forcing a smile. "Thank you." She moved away into the crowd quickly, heading for the double doors along one side that led out to the balcony. She burst through them into the cool October air, taking huge draughts of air as she clung to the metal railing. Slowly she calmed, gaining some embarrassment along with her composure when she noticed several lusty couples in the shadows near the wall that were taking full advantage of the dark.

"Debbie?"

Debbie turned uneasily. Henry stood there, dressed as a captain of some kind. Gold brocade was across his chest and on his shoulders, but his head was bare.

Great. Just what she didn't need. "Hello, Henry," Debbie said automatically, discreetly looking for the easiest exit back to the party.

"May I talk to you?"

"I don't think there is anything to talk about." Debbie moved to brush past him, but he grabbed her arm.

"Please," Henry said. "Just a few moments."

Debbie stopped and waited, arms folded.

'It was hard for me, the night you told me no," Henry said, uncomfortable. "Especially what you admitted. I guess I always put you up on a pedestal. I never thought that—"

"If you have something to say, say it," Debbie said angrily. "I don't need to hear you go over my past sins."

"I'm just saying it's taken me a while to understand what's important," Henry said. "You're important, Debbie." He went to one knee, extending a box in his hand. "And I want you to be my wife."

Oh shit. Debbie looked down at him, his face so earnest, knowing she only had a minute at most to come up with some kind of reply. But what?

Tell him this is sudden, Shaker said in her mind. *Tell him you'll have to think about it. Cry a little if you can, and kiss him. It'll buy time.*

Debbie took the box. The ring was easily two carats, with one-carat emeralds on either side. Stunning, in short. "I don't know what to say."

"Say yes," Henry prodded. "I'll make you happy, Debbie. I promise."

"I'm stunned," Debbie said, stepping back from him. "Really, I thought you'd moved on."

"I couldn't," Henry said, getting to his feet with some effort. He smiled. "Bad knees, I'm afraid. But the rest of me works fine."

I'll bet it does, Shaker said in Debbie's mind. Debbie cleared her throat hastily, covering her urge to grin.

"I love you," Henry said devotedly. "Will you marry me?"

"I can't give you an answer," Debbie said as gently as she could manage. "Not when two minutes ago I thought you hated me."

"I don't hate you," Henry said, flushing, appalled. "How could you think that, Debbie? I love you—"

"I understand that," Debbie placated. "But I am going to need some time to sort out my feelings for you. I don't want to say yes without knowing it's right for me." She caressed his cheek. "I need to be able to know I'd make you happy, too."

"I know you will." Henry grabbed her and kissed her, his passion swallowing her in its fervor until she was kissing Henry back with equal vigor.

Mistress...Earth to Mistress, Shaker said in her mind.

Remembering herself, Debbie pulled away, breathing hard. "Will you give me time?"

"If you'll wear the ring until you decide," Henry said.

Debbie slipped it on her finger. It was a perfect fit. "All right."

"When can I expect an answer?" Henry asked lovingly.

"Christmas," Debbie said finally. "By Christmas."

Henry kissed her once more, then led her inside. "Do you want to dance?" he asked.

Debbie was saved from answering with the appearance of an angry Dante, who grabbed hold of Henry's arm. "What is this?" he accused. "No wonder I haven't been able to get anywhere. You're screwing her!"

"You're drunk," Henry said calmly, removing Dante's hand. "Now leave—"

Dante punched Henry, knocking the older man backward. Henry fell against a table of desserts, which wobbled but didn't topple. Other guests hurried to get out of the way as Dante grabbed hold of his jacket, preparing to punch the dazed man again.

"Stop." Shaker grabbed hold of Dante's fist as it descended, stopping him cold.

Dante turned, then shook Shaker off without a trace of fear. "Get lost. This doesn't concern you."

"What about Martin?" Shaker rumbled low, a small smile curving his lips. "He concerns you."

Dante's eyes widened, and he stumbled backward. Turning so fast he nearly fell then ran for the exit. His fairy date watched him go with shocked eyes, cursed, then took out her phone and began texting.

"I'm sorry," Debbie said, helping Henry to his feet. "Are you okay?"

"Yes, with the intercession of this big guy," Henry said in a thankful tone. He held out his hand to Shaker. "I don't believe we've met. I'm Henry."

"I go by Shake," Shaker said happily, shaking Henry's hand. "At least in the sequel to *Smoke and Ashes*. What do you think of the costume?"

"Honestly," Henry said contritely. "It's been done a lot, the black horns and red skin. The loincloth's good, though. It looks authentic."

"Thanks," Shaker said with a grin. "Pandora's costume department outdid themselves. I think it looks like real human skin—"

"We…um, I should be going," Debbie said, kissing Henry's cheek.

"Yes," Henry said with a loving look at Debbie. "I'll take you home." He reached to take her arm.

"Sorry," Sheila said, swooping in and blocking him. "Debbie is coming home with me for a girl's night, Henry."

Henry looked crestfallen. He turned to Debbie with a questioning expression.

"I did say I would," Debbie chimed in quickly. "Besides, I need some time, like I said."

"All right," Henry said. He kissed Debbie on the lips, then stepped back as Sheila led her away.

* * * *

"God, that was close," Sheila said, flopping down with wet hair on her long sectional couch. She put her feet up, then took another sip of wine.

"How many times do I have to ask you not to mention the G-word?" Harp said irritably. "I've been after you for months."

"And no JC, either," Song added. "Gives us all a headache."

"Sorry," Sheila said apologetically. "It's all that parochial schooling."

"Sheila, what am I going to do?" Debbie said. She was pacing the floor back and forth. "Henry proposed." She looked again at her ring finger, examining the sparkling rocks.

"What do you want to do?" Sheila asked.

"Yes, Mistress," Shaker intoned from the doorway. "What do you want to do?"

Debbie darted a look at him, then away. "I'm not sure," she admitted. "But I'm afraid if I say no, he won't help me with that stock."

"Go ahead and marry him," Song said with a shrug. "I don't see the problem. You can always do away with him later."

"I don't want to 'do away' with Henry," Debbie said angrily. "Which is precisely why I wish he'd never proposed! I don't want him involved with any of this!"

"It sounds as if you have feelings for him, my Mistress," Shaker said.

"It doesn't matter what my feelings are," Debbie said, exasperated. "What matters is that my life is a certain way. I'm not sure that I want it to change. Henry is going to expect a wife, and I'm not sure I want to be a wife."

"Don't forget brats," Song added. "Human men always want get of their own."

"Look," Sheila said loudly. "Harp and Song have some good points, but it boils down to what you want to do, Debbie. If you marry Henry, it is going to change your life, and probably our friendship. Personally, I'm telling you not to do it." Her tone softened. "If you loved him, you'd be thrilled that he asked you, and you aren't. So tell him no and let the deal with the stock fall apart. It's not worth trying to string him along until that's done. Besides, I still think he has a screw loose for all of his weird behavior."

"No, the passion is there," Shaker said, coming forward to Debbie. "I felt it through our bond when he kissed you."

Because no one has kissed me in a while, Debbie retorted to him mentally. *That's all it was.*

Oh, really? Shaker replied, his eyebrows rising. *Then I suppose I'll have to correct that.*

"Do you love him?" Sheila asked Debbie, taking her by the shoulders.

"I don't know," Debbie said, her eyes sliding away.

Sheila's eyes narrowed. "Why won't you let me in? I'm your friend. How can I help you decide what to do if you won't tell me how you really feel?"

"Because it doesn't matter how I feel!" Debbie shouted, shoving her away. "Not about any of this!"

"It does matter," Sheila persisted. "You shouldn't marry someone you don't love."

"Love is overrated," Harp muttered. "What you need to look for is someone who likes the same food and TV shows."

"Shh," Song hissed at him. "We're being serious."

"I am serious," Harp replied more loudly. "How many humans have we lost over the years lately to their spouses killing them? And for what? It's always because they couldn't watch one more episode of *Survivor* or

121

eat one more vegetarian tofu meal without cracking!"

"Sheila, I need some time to sort out what I'm going to do," Debbie said. She motioned to Shaker. "I'm going home. I'll see you on Monday at the office."

"What about our proposed party?" Harp said plaintively, stroking his harp. "I wanted to play for you—"

Debbie took Shaker's hand, and he teleported them instantly, cutting off whatever else Harp had been saying. She headed into her bedroom without a word. Shaker followed her, slamming the door closed behind him.

Debbie turned to him. "Get out."

Shaker grabbed her. "Not until I'm done filling your void." He kissed her.

Debbie slapped him hard. Shaker snarled at her, then let her go. "What do you want from me?" he said.

Debbie sat down on the bed, and didn't answer. Shaker looked down at her for a moment, then sat down beside her.

"Marry him if you want to," Shaker said finally. "I told you it's not a problem."

"What you say and the truth are often very different things," Debbie said wearily. She wiped at her eyes.

Shaker tipped her head up, so she was forced to look at him. "Why are you crying?"

Debbie closed her eyes, so she wouldn't have to look into his. "Because I'm scared."

"Scared of what?"

"Scared that what I said to Sheila is true." Debbie pulled away, and dabbed at her eyes with the edge of her sheet. "I'm scared that I've done so much for Pandora and that I'm going to lose it anyway. I'm scared of opening myself to someone and getting burned."

"Henry seems to be a good man," Shaker said. "Even if he's no fighter."

"Being a fighter isn't everything," Debbie said irritably.

"Oh, really?" Shaker said, standing up and facing her. "I don't think you'd have found me half so attractive these past months if I'd neglected to fight your battles for you."

"I wouldn't have needed anyone to fight battles for me without you instigating the attacks on me in the first place!" Debbie yelled at him.

Shaker glared at her, then disappeared.

Debbie slumped down on her bed, wiping at her eyes again. Her efforts smeared her Joker makeup, causing burning and stinging when it got into her eyes. Swearing, she went into the bathroom and took a long hot shower, scrubbing herself pink. Emerging into the chilly bathroom, she wrapped a towel around herself, then looked hard into the half-steamed mirror.

Yes, the priest had tried to kill her because of Shaker. But she'd never have even made it that far if Shaker hadn't saved her from Rebecca's curse.

The thoughts weren't from Shaker. They were just her own guilty conscience. God, what she wouldn't give for some advice from someone who was not only informed and intelligent, but also impartial…

Debbie stopped still, struck by sudden inspiration, then dressed hurriedly. She hurried to the garage, saying a quick prayer.

* * * *

The night was cool and silent. The brick building loomed above her, making her feel small. Debbie went to the door and tried to open it, but the door wouldn't budge.

It was close to midnight on Halloween. Maybe churches closed? Debbie rapped hard on the door. "Hello?"

"He will not hear you," a child's small voice said. "You're a filthy murderer."

Debbie turned, then let out a shriek. A foggy child stood there, glaring at her with black holes for eyes. A familiar looking child she'd never met in the flesh. "Celia. You...you're dead."

"You killed her. You killed my mother."

"No," Debbie said, her rational words squeaking with fear. "I didn't hurt Amanda. I never killed anyone. I—"

The thing moved closer. "Demon whore," it hissed. "Sins come home to roost. There is no safety for you here." It reached out ghostly fingers with long white claws, then swiped at her. One sharp talon connected, the pain searing as it laid open the top of Debbie's hand.

Debbie screamed again, then threw her purse at the thing. It passed right through, spilling its contents all over the parking lot pavement.

"You are evil," the thing hissed, reaching back its arm to strike. "Your torment is deserved—"

Debbie screamed again, cowering. There was a sudden hiss, the sounds of tearing metal, and then a wail of fury as the ghost dissolved. The white fog dissipated as suddenly as it had appeared, leaving Debbie blinking up at a small figure in black that was sheathing his serrated knife.

"Mr. Lash?" Debbie stammered.

"It's just Lash," the figure replied casually.

"What are you doing here?"

"What any sane person would be doing coming to church this time of night," Lash hissed at her, even as he offered her a hand up. "Getting my knives blessed and stocking up on holy water, of course. I can't very well do it in the light of day with the children and old ladies, can I? What the fuck are you doing here this time of night? Looking for absolution?"

She had been, but there was no way she'd admit that to him. "I wanted a blessed knife," Debbie stammered.

Lash studied her. "If you're thinking to surprise Shaker some night with a gelding, let me advise you against it, little girl."

"Why do you have to be such an asshole?" Debbie grumbled, kneeling and scooping up her scattered belongings.

"Why do you have to be human?" Lash replied with a laugh. "I'll change if you will."

Debbie suppressed a chill, remembering that Lash was some kind of snake man. She hurriedly knelt and grabbed the rest of her things, shoving them haphazardly back into her purse. Standing, she faced Lash, who was still watching her. "Thanks for saving me," she said awkwardly, then turned to walk away.

Lash grabbed her arm, his strength surprising for his size. "What about my movie?" he asked. "You guys cast any parts yet? Or do you have to have Dev's money first?"

We haven't even agreed to do any weresnake movie, only the vampire one. "We just got the paperwork from Devlin," Debbie replied. "There was no mention in it about your idea, as I recall."

"As you recall?" Lash said sarcastically. "There wouldn't be though, would there? My movie was going to be something separate, as I recall. Your partner said it was a good idea." His eyes narrowed. "Or were you just stringing me along, you and your pal?"

Yes. But his knife might find another victim if she admitted that here and now. "Is this some kind of threat?" Debbie said bluntly. "Or are you looking to get paid for saving me with a film?"

Lash took his hand off her, shifting his weight slightly. "No," he said in a calmer tone. "I want this to be completely legit. But I also wanted to get things rolling, so I thought I should ask, since you were here and everything."

She could manage this. "We're working on the idea," Debbie said carefully.

"Do you need any help?" Lash hissed, stressing the last word and drawing it out. "I don't want this to be one of those pictures that stays an idea, if you get my drift."

He's serious about this. Fuck. "First, we'd need a good script," Debbie said slowly. "Sheila's looking into those. Then we'd have to buy rights to it, then work out a budget, then decide on a rating, and a bunch of other things. Casting would be one of the last things before we began shooting the actual film. Films take a lot of time to put together even when the script is all set to go, there is a budget, and most of the cast lined up, Lash. So far we don't have anything, but we're working on it, believe me."

Lash stared at her, then nodded. "All right. But keep me in the loop, okay? I want regular updates. You can call through Dev's phone. I can help if you can't find financing. I've got money of my own."

What kind of money could he possibly have? He's just some kind of bodyguard. Debbie stared at him, thinking furiously. "Okay," she said finally. "But I need a favor in return."

"I think I just did you a favor, woman," Lash smirked. "That revenant was about to slice you up good."

"Revenant? You mean the ghost girl?"

"That was no girl," Lash said coolly. "That was a specter and it finding you wasn't no accident...um, any accident. Someone sent it after you." He took out his serrated knife, showing her the shiny blade. "My

125

knife is blessed, so it sent the thing back to Hell. Holy water would have done the same."

"Shaker said you have to have faith for that to work," Debbie murmured.

"Someone's faith, for sure," Lash said, nodding. "The priest here is good about that. He considers helping me as part of God's plan. His blessing lasts through several kills usually."

"What if the thing comes back, and you aren't there to stab it again?" Debbie said stridently. "I need some kind of protection. Can you help me or not?"

Lash muttered something under his breath, then took several throwing stars out of his pocket. He handed them to Debbie, who felt the slightest spark when the metal touched her palm. "These are blessed, too," he said. "You can likely feel it, being demon-bound yourself. Consider them on loan, until you get your own."

"What good are these going to do me?" Debbie said skeptically, staring at the sharp little metal stars. "They're teeny."

"They'll slow a demon down enough for you to get away," Lash replied. "Every second counts. You'd never be able to knife fight one and win, trust me. If you don't take a demon by surprise, usually you've already lost."

Lash had been here getting knives blessed and stocking up on holy water. "You hunt demons?"

"No," Lash hissed tiredly. "I sometimes get hunted. And we're done here, Debbie. You should get back to your demon protector before that revenant returns. I can't fuck about here all night telling you things you should already know. I've got things to do." He strode away.

"Wait!" she called, but Lash had already melted into the darkness, leaving her alone.

Chapter Eleven

~ November ~

What was she going to do?

Nearly a week had passed, and Debbie was no closer to making a decision about Henry. But she did enjoy how the ring sparkled on her finger. Several coworkers had noticed it, but Debbie had only smiled at their eager questions, and walked away. She looked again at the ring, admiring it in the wan sunlight filtering in through her dirty window. It would be so much easier not to wear it. But it was too beautiful...

"If you can tear yourself away from the sparkling rock," Sheila said from the doorway. "I have some piracy issues of our own to deal with."

Debbie grimaced. "Not Dante again?"

Sheila shook her head. "No, this is more a problem with someone getting a copy of the final version of *Smoke and Ashes*. They posted it to the internet on a free site. We pulled it down before it got noticed, thanks to some quick alerts that our IT people had put in place. Song and Harp are taking care of it now, as this quarter's favor."

"If you have the culprit and all copies, plus a system that lets us know immediately when this kind of thing happens, why the glum face?"

"Because it shouldn't have happened," Sheila said, making a face at Debbie. "I hired most of the new people in the department, and it's probably one of them. We've never had trouble before with piracy."

"We also never had any movies before worth pirating," Debbie said with a smile. "Success has its drawbacks."

"Maybe you're right," Sheila said, stretching. "Are you ready for our appointment at the Black Rose?"

"Yes," Debbie said eagerly. "Let me pack up and get my coat."

Sheila left, and Debbie began putting files in her satchel. Lately, there was just so much to go through. Sheila had given her three new possible weresnake movies—written for werewolves, but Sheila assured Debbie they could be modified to work for a snakelike creature—and ten new scripts that she was considering obtaining. All of them were supernatural, but of varying genres. After *Hell's Gate's* rating problem, Sheila had said she wasn't comfortable purchasing a script without a second opinion. Debbie had agreed, even if it made the workload that much harder. Even with low-pressure investors like Mrs. Triss and Devlin, Debbie still wanted to make sure they had a good return on their money.

There was also a complete file on the stock plan, the implementation of which was coming up fast. Henry hadn't pushed her yet for an answer on their personal business, but he and she had been meeting once a week to prepare for the deal. Truthfully, Debbie wondered that it couldn't be done without so many meetings, or Henry's endless explanations of how stock worked, who would be running the board, their qualifications, their proposed duties and work schedule, when regular meetings would be held, etc., etc. Yet she also appreciated Henry's keeping her informed of each step of the process, because having been in all of those meetings with him, Debbie confirmed that not only was Henry's plan solid, but it was completely legal.

Dante had not been thrilled to find out he was not inheriting the lion's share of the stock from his parents' estate, of course. Several meetings now with Mr. Catarella had been to deal with Rebecca's will, and the allocation of her assets. Dante had been livid when he found out that Debbie and he now had equal shares in Pandora. He'd made it clear that he was going to be the one to buy the stock when Titan released it, even though Henry had assured her time and time again that wouldn't be allowed to happen…

"Deb," Sheila called from the doorway. "Come on, we're going to be late!"

"Wait," a male voice called. Mr. Catarella barged into the office.

"Ms. Deal, I need to talk to you."

Debbie smiled, long-suffering. "I suppose it can't wait until Monday?"

"No, I'm sorry. But it won't take long, promise."

Debbie glanced over at Sheila. "Go ahead. I'll be there shortly."

Sheila looked as if she wasn't certain she should leave, but Mr. Catarella shut the door firmly in her face, then handed Debbie a file. "You need to see this."

Debbie looked over the copies of emails, her face whitening with rage. "Jett Black is our leak for the pirated copy of *Smoke and Ashes*?"

Mr. Catarella nodded. "IT confirmed it was his copy that ended up on that free internet site."

"Why?"

"Money," Mr. Catarella said simply. "Look at the last page in that file. You'll see he was paid five thousand dollars for it. I'm sure you'll recognize the name of the buyer."

"Titan Pictures," Debbie said in disbelief. "Why would they be so stupid to leave this kind of trail?"

"That employee who brokered the deal is no longer an employee," Mr. Catarella said meaningfully. "He was fired the very next day, after he sent that email. According to Titan, they fired him because of gross misconduct. Yet he somehow retained his benefits and got a severance package with a year's worth of pay. After signing a non-disclosure agreement, of course."

"So they covered their tracks," Debbie surmised.

Mr. Catarella nodded. "We can sue them, but the most we'll get back is that five thou., which is likely what our legal expenses would be just to sue. Plus any kind of lawsuit will be sure to pull in Jett Black, who will probably be the one the media will choose to spotlight. There is no way we won't either look like the witless victim, or the unfeeling corporate bad guys who care more about their bottom line than a man's health."

Even though Pandora was neither. "Have you talked to him?" Debbie asked. "I know we don't pay as much as the big houses, but why would he risk this for five thousand dollars? You said he wasn't healthy?"

"My understanding is that he is addicted to painkillers since his skiing accident a few months ago," the lawyer said candidly. "But he may have been addicted longer than that. We don't offer employees a drug abuse program, and he can't foot the bill a second time, as he's already flunked out of rehab once. I know we're in a sensitive position with him being our biggest star. But if we don't get rid of him, he'll just do this again the next time his cash supply runs low."

No, he won't, Debbie thought. *Shaker, do something to him so he loses his crutch, permanently...but can still work for us.*

Short of possessing him, there isn't much I can do, Shaker replied. *Drug addicts are notorious for not responding to threats or personal danger.*

Then possess him for a while, and see how that goes? Debbie thought.

Thy will be done, Shaker responded.

"There is something else as well," Mr. Catarella said. "I believe that your fiancé has not been entirely truthful with you."

Debbie narrowed her eyes. "How do you know about my fiancé?"

Mr. Catarella smiled, baring shark teeth. "Let's say we have a mutual friend with a taste for tanning leather. He asked me to look into the legal aspects for you."

Shaker? Debbie thought. *Is this true?*

I thought it wise, Shaker replied. *You were so worried about the deal. Catarella's good, too. He was a powerful lawyer before he became demon. Don't worry, he's not looking for anything but to be a help.*

"What did you find?" Debbie asked the lawyer. He produced a sheet of paper, which he handed to her.

"I already knew this," Debbie said slowly, scanning the paper. "Henry is working to take the company public."

"He's given himself authority to set the share price."

"Only for the initial deal, I thought," Debbie said, confused. "Why would that matter?"

"Because if he can set the share price, he can use information asymmetry to cause the price to go falsely low."

"He wants to be able to sell it to me cheaply before Dante can get his hands on it. Why should that matter?"

"Because I don't think Henry's planning to sell to you or Dante," Mr. Catarella said darkly. "I believe he's going to sell the stock to Titan, who will then partner with Dante to force you to sign that contract so Titan can seize Pandora."

"Why?" Debbie managed, her throat suddenly dry. "Why would he do that?"

"Because he's built his fortune orchestrating takeover deals like this for Titan over the years," Mr. Catarella said. "Gloom Pictures, Harry Heimlin's Productions, Vertigo Pictures, Bene Studios, and dozens more. All disappeared and are now part of Titan. Vertigo Pictures was a similar deal to Pandora's proposed one. He's going to do it again."

Debbie wanted to cry, to scream, to rip the ring she'd stared at all week off her finger. But something was still off. *Henry's confession had been so heartfelt that night. And why propose if he was only going to betray her? None of it made any sense.*

"I drafted a letter firing Henry, to stall his efforts," the lawyer said. "If you sign it, that will temporarily stop him from pushing the deal through. But taking back Henry's legal rights is going to be a battle, especially as soon as he knows we know what he's planning."

Debbie grabbed a pen from her desk. *Should she sign or no? Henry had given her no reason not to trust him.*

Song appeared before Debbie. Startling her with a loud cry, she grabbed hold of Debbie. "Sheila's hurt! You have to come quick!"

Debbie scrawled a signature, handed the paper to the lawyer, and grabbed hold of Song's hand, calling for Shaker to come as fast as he could.

* * * *

Debbie stood by the bed, clutching Sheila's hand. The flesh was smooth and pink, unlike the other 90% of her body that was red as demon skin. Her friend was unconscious, breathing shallowly under the towel that covered her torso.

"The mud wrap…there was something in it," Song said. "I felt her burning. I got here and wiped it off, but I couldn't get it off fast enough."

"I killed the woman, Vivian," Harp said vindictively. "She didn't know anything. She was only following orders to kill the woman she'd

131

been hired to serve since the first of this year."

Debbie stared at him in horror.

"Yes," Harp said. "She thought Sheila was you."

A big man burst in, crossing fast to Debbie and hugging her. *It's me, Mistress,* Shaker said in her mind. The man drew back from her. Debbie was looking into the handsome chiseled face of Jett Black. "I came as soon as I heard," he said. "What happened?"

"A trap was set for Debbie," Song said sorrowfully. "And our Mistress tripped it instead."

"A man usually works here with her," Debbie said to Song and Harp. "He would have been here to handle me. Damn it, I forgot his name—"

"I've seen the one you speak of. I'll get him," Harp said.

"Bring him alive," Shaker instructed, looking Sheila over. "We need to know who was behind this."

Harp nodded, then disappeared.

"She needs magic healing or she'll die. Song, take us to my brother," Shaker said, clasping Debbie's hand. Song picked up Sheila's limp form, then clasped Debbie's other hand in her free one.

They appeared in a dark earthen room, with strong light. Bottles lined the shelves along most of the walls, except for a line of books and a pile of tattered scrolls. There were several easy chairs, a floor lamp, and a few tables, one of them resembling a medical table near the far wall.

"Titus! Leri!" Shaker yelled. "Come quick!"

There was some creaking of stairs, then another demon walked into the room. He looked similar in feature to Shaker, from the waist up. He was dressed in jeans, with bare feet. "Who are you wearing, brother?"

"It's not important," Shaker replied, helping Song lay Sheila down on the medical table. "We need your healing skills, Titus."

Titus came close to Sheila, lifting the towels and looking over her burns. "Bad, for a human," he intoned. "She won't last long. This is liquid Hellfire, and it's still burning inward—"

"Can you help her?" Debbie said frantically. "Please, you have to help her!"

Titus looked over at Debbie, then at Shaker.

"This one is ours, brother," Shaker said. "The injured woman is

Song's Mistress, Sheila."

"Yes," Song said meekly. "Please help her, Master Titus."

"I'll pay you," Debbie urged. "Please, do what you can."

"She's important to Devlin," Shaker added.

Titus shot Shaker a grumpy stare, then began assembling bottles. "Get me the Darkfriend's Helper. It's the green small book in Greek on the second shelf, near the far end."

Shaker hurried to comply as Titus tore back the sheet from Sheila's smoking body. Sheila stirred, moaning in pain as Titus began pouring some clear concoction on her from a large jar. She began to twitch, her red skin blistering up as the liquid flowed over it.

"What are you doing?" Debbie cried.

"The only thing that stops Hellfire is holy water," Titus said, continuing to douse Sheila a she began writhing. "I'm going to have to immerse her, maybe even open up the deeper burns. She's going to be screaming before we're done. Then will come the healing, if she survives the removal."

"Removal?"

"I'm going to have to take most of her skin off," Titus said. "Down to the second layer, at least. Maybe deeper."

How would Sheila look, even if she survived this? Debbie swallowed hard. "Can't you do anything for the pain?"

"Not until I get the Hellfire off," Titus said, glancing over at Debbie. "You must have some nasty enemies. Of the many painful ways to die, this is in the top ten."

Henry. How could he have done this?

Mistress, you may want to leave, Shaker said in her mind. *This will be an ordeal of suffering for her. I can come and get you when it's done.*

And what if Sheila didn't survive it? Debbie bit her lip, then grasped Sheila's hand. "Do it."

"Are you sure you want to stay?" Titus asked, lifting up another jar of holy water and beginning to pour. Sheila's screams resumed louder than before.

"She's my friend," Debbie said bitterly, wiping at her tears. "I have to."

* * * *

Debbie was roused by a nudge from Shaker, his new human face at odds with his familiar body language. She was sitting in one of the chairs in the demon's basement laboratory. The smell of sulfur and burnt meat was strong enough to make her gag with her first breath. Debbie coughed, then took a deep breath though her mouth.

"She's healed," Shaker said gently. "Titus gave her something for the pain and she's sleeping."

"Will she be okay?"

"The first layer of skin will regrow by tonight," Titus said from the opposite chair, where he was reading a book. "By Monday, you might not be able to tell she was ever burned." He smiled, showing no teeth. "I think she'll make a full recovery."

"How can I thank you?" Debbie said gratefully.

"With payment, of course," a melodic voice said. Devlin walked in, dressed in a white linen suit. "Sorry to see you in such circumstances, my dear. You must have some bad enemies."

Debbie stared at the vampire. *Had he done it so they'd be indebted to him and make his damned movie?*

Not a chance, Shaker replied. *Devlin would have killed you both already if he was going to. And he's not hurting for money, Mistress.*

"I like Sheila. Who did this?" Devlin asked, looking at everyone in turn.

Say nothing, Shaker cautioned Debbie. *Devlin is very angry, though he may not look or sound it.*

Debbie went to Sheila's side, looking at her friend. She was sleeping peacefully, her face bright pink as if with sunburn. Debbie grasped her hand and squeezed. "You're going to be okay."

"I found the boy," Harp said to Devlin, coming forward caked with dried blood from the direction of the stairs. "He said that the order was a standing one, that they'd waited all year for Debbie to come in alone. This was the first time she did."

"How could he confuse us?" Debbie said angrily. "He knows what we look like!"

Harp shook his head. "On the contrary, the boy who hurt Sheila was only hired this month. They fired the previous one because he wasn't friendly enough to customers. Luckily, he was so horrified by what had happened he didn't run. I found him drunk in his house with the shades drawn."

"You know he did it?" Devlin asked.

How could the guy apply that Liquid Hellfire? Wouldn't it burn him, too? Debbie thought to Shaker.

Probably bespelled gloves, Shaker replied. *He likely said an incantation to activate the hellfire after it was applied. But you're right that this was a complex spell, something a witch would usually not have access to.*

Harp nodded at Devlin. "He had been told to find a way to apply a special jar of mud if the blond woman named Debbie ever came in alone. Sheila came in alone, her hair was blond, and the account you share is still in your name—"

"It matters less who applied it or how than who ordered it done," Shaker interrupted. "I'm done with games. Did you find the owner of the Black Rose?"

"Yes," Harp nodded. "And he gave up all his secrets before I killed him, even ones I didn't ask for."

Could he waste any more time telling them what they needed to know? "Who did this to Sheila?" Debbie yelled. "Was it Henry?"

"Dante," Harp said. "The owner said he had paid for the package of treatments, and supplied the special mud." He looked over at Sheila and Debbie. "I saw his memories. He didn't lie. It was Dante."

"So Dante is allied with a witch, at the very least," Devlin mused. "We'll need to kill her before going after him."

"It's not a witch," Shaker corrected hesitantly. "Dante's ally is a demon."

Everyone stared at Shaker. "One you are loathe to tangle with yourself," Devlin supplied.

"I don't need Azaroth as an enemy," Shaker said defensively. "Neither do you."

"And your failure to act allowed Sheila to be hurt," Devlin countered.

Shaker stared back at him without the slightest guilt. "Dante has made mistake after mistake with his demon, and the police already have linked him to two murders. With the plan that Debbie had to secure the stock, I thought we had less than a month to wait until he lost control and attacked her directly. Then the police could be manipulated into killing Dante, and Azaroth would be sent back to Hell."

"He's right, Devlin," Titus said in a low tone. "That demons do not sabotage one another is an unwritten rule. To do so usually means you spend the rest of your existence fighting that demon and all his allies. I do not want to be on Hell's revolving door." He looked at Shaker. "You're sure that Dante is about to crack?"

Shaker nodded. "Yes. And I've gone to significant trouble to make sure that once he does, our troubles will be over."

Devlin looked from Titus to Shaker. "Very well." He stood reluctantly. "Make sure that Sheila has enough paste to finish her healing, Titus, before Harp and Song take her home."

"Wait," Debbie called angrily after him. "That's it? You're not going to do anything about this? Sheila nearly died!"

Mistress, Shaker cautioned. *Do not provoke him.*

Devlin turned back to Debbie, then in the next instant he had hold of her. Debbie tried to back up, but the vampire was already there, gripping her arms as she flailed. "Do not question me," he said, his golden eyes tinged with red. "I am sorry that happened to your friend, but I am not going to go to war for you, or for her. Not when waiting a few weeks will give us a much better solution no one had to bleed for."

Debbie opened her mouth to swear at him, to tell him he could screw himself, that he could take his money and shove it, because she'd never make his damned movie. But Shaker shut her mouth. Her words came out as angry grunts as she struggled, her face contorting wildly as she tried to open her lips.

Devlin let her go abruptly, and Debbie stumbled back, grabbing the table for support. Sheila let out a mild groan at the table shaking, but didn't wake.

"There is still the matter of payment for what Titus did to heal Sheila," Devlin said coldly. "Magical healing of this level is very expensive. While Sheila can pay most of what is owed when she is well again, I will require something from your company as well, Debbie."

Again, Debbie fought to tell him to go to hell, and again, Shaker stopped her. *Stay silent.*

"I want complete control over the picture," Devlin announced. He went to a nearby table, and picked up a sheaf of pages clipped together, and handed it to her. "There is the script, including my ideas for locations." He smiled cruelly. "Find unknowns for the actors. I have included descriptions of most of the cast on the first page, for your costume and makeup departments." He chuckled. "I'm sure you'll have trouble finding someone who looks like me with the right color eyes. Make sure you get contact lenses for him that approximate my eye color, including versions with a red tinge, for the violent scenes. Adieu." He strode away, the stairs creaking as he ascended.

Debbie was still grunting angrily when Shaker took her hand and teleported her back to her house. As they appeared in her living room. Shaker withdrew his control over her voice.

"Son of a bitch!" Debbie screeched, rounding on Shaker. "Why didn't you fucking do something?"

"Do what?" Shaker grumbled, going for the liquor cabinet. "Unless you don't care about your star actor Jett being marked up, I'm going to have to take a backseat to any hand to hand fighting." He poured two glasses of wine. "Not that I could have done anything, anyway."

"You could have punched him," Debbie said angrily.

"To what end?" Shaker said. He knocked back his wine in one swallow. "I don't fight my brother, Debbie. Ever. And Titus would be bound to respond if I attacked Devlin."

"I'm not making his damned movie," Debbie said vehemently.

"Yes, we are," Shaker replied. He poured another glass, then handed one to Debbie. "Drink up."

Debbie considered smashing it, but then took a swallow. She set down the glass, then began to pace.

"I don't understand why you're so agitated," Shaker commented as he watched her walking back and forth. "Sheila will be fine. And as I said, Dante is going to come to grief soon enough. Remember that man Martin I mentioned to Dante at the party, when I pulled him off Henry? Dante had Martin killed. That Detective O'Hara that came to see you knows Dante had something to do with the man's death. He's assembling evidence right now."

"Won't Dante's demon block that?" Debbie asked angrily. "I've been so dumb. I wondered why you didn't want to go after Dante directly. You never really said why, but it's because he's had Azaroth all along."

"Yes, Azaroth can arrange for evidence to disappear," Shaker affirmed, "and he's done so already a few times, on Dante's orders. But that also plays into our hands. At this point, the detective knows Dante is guilty, Debbie. He knows it but can't prove it, and Dante's been arrogant as hell about that, like he is with everything else. When the time comes, O'Hara won't hesitate to shoot Dante dead, instead of wound him—"

"I want him dead now." Debbie stalked angrily to the bedroom, then began undressing. "He's been a thorn in my side all year! What good is a demon afraid to fight?"

"See, I told you that you only cared about someone to fight for you," Shaker said mockingly. "You American females, you're all the same. Always overeager to see a fistfight for your favors."

Debbie ignored him.

"And what about Henry?" Shaker asked, watching her take off her clothes.

Debbie didn't answer him, stripping off the rumpled blouse and slacks.

"I heard what the lawyer Catarella told you," Shaker continued. "I guess this puts the wedding on hold—"

"Get out," Debbie said tiredly. "I'm in no mood for your bullshit tonight."

Shaker didn't answer. Debbie turned, wondering if he had gone, but he was still there, watching her.

"I told you to get out," Debbie screamed at him.

"I'm sorry," Shaker said softly, the timbre of his voice Jett's sexy tones.

"No, you aren't," Debbie said, turning away. "You'd just like some sex now that I'm close to naked."

In a moment, Shaker was behind her. But instead of the sexy touch she expected, he reached to grab her hand instead, threading his human fingers through hers. "I am sorry, Mistress. I don't want anyone to hurt you. But I didn't come this far to lose what we've built." He squeezed her hand gently. "Not when my way will finish Dante and his demon for good. You asked me before if all demons were as reasonable as I am. Trust me that this is the best way to assure that when Azaroth is done with Dante, we will not have to deal with him again."

Debbie didn't answer. Shaker slowly turned her to face him, then hugged her close. Debbie tried to remain rigid, but as he rubbed her back lightly, she relaxed into him, hugging him.

"Do you like me better," Shaker said hesitantly. "Like this?"

Debbie looked up at him in surprise. His expression was serious, and more than a little hopeful. "You mean without the hooves?"

Shaker nodded.

Debbie ran her eyes over Jett's body: tall, muscular but not too bulging, jet black lustrous hair with a slight curl, easy smile with dimples, chiseled jaw and cheekbones, bedroom eyes of bright blue, and clear tanned skin.

Shaker laughed, relieved. "You don't have to say anything. I can feel your lust."

Debbie smiled. "Why did you ask, if you already knew?"

Shaker blinked, then seemed not to know where to look. "I don't possess people as a rule," he said finally. He moved past her to the mirror, looking at his appearance, then began to unbutton his shirt.

"Why not?" Debbie said curiously, even as she watched hungrily as each button came free, showing more and more of his chest.

"My Mistresses don't usually ask me to," Shaker admitted, glancing back at Debbie. He slipped out of his shirt, then looked at himself again in the mirror, turning this way and that. "He's not too bad. But he could use a haircut."

"I like it longer," Debbie said, touching the long black waves. "You cut it, and millions of fans are going to be disappointed for *Smoke and Ashes II*."

Shaker rolled his eyes. Then he began to strip off his pants. "Might as well see the package."

Debbie watched, curious to see what would be revealed. Jett had refused to do any scene without jeans, though many of his scenes in *Smoke and Ashes* had him walking around shirtless.

"Hmm," Shaker said, peering into his boxers. Then he walked into the bathroom.

Not to be stymied, Debbie followed him. But Shaker had disappeared. *Get back here, now!* Debbie thought. *I want to see, too.*

Shaker didn't answer.

Grumbling, Debbie turned on the shower, undressed the rest of the way, and lost herself under the hot spray.

Chapter Twelve

~ December ~

Where was that damned demon? Debbie called again mentally for Shaker, but there was no answer. She hadn't seen him for a week now. Trying to contact "Jett" at his home also hadn't worked. He had apparently called in and said he'd be out all week, that he was fighting some bad flu. Debbie knew it was a lie, yet she didn't want to track Shaker down and force a confrontation.

You're just afraid of finding him with someone else. Jett was a regular party animal, or so the tabloids said. He probably had a live-in lover, maybe several...

Debbie shook off the thought, then got up and went down the hall in search of Sheila. The VP was at her desk, reading a script amidst stacks of papers.

"How are you?" Debbie said, after a perfunctory knock.

"Fine, if you'd stop asking me five times a day," Sheila replied with a smile. "I'm feeling fine, really, Deb."

I was just worried. "I'm glad. Do you want to go to lunch?"

"Can't," Sheila said. "I told Dev I'd read that script he gave you and give him feedback by tonight."

"Dev?" Debbie said innocently.

Sheila blushed heavily. "So he asked me to call him that. So what?"

Had a little roll in the sack and a lovebite been part of Dev's price for the healing? Debbie was too embarrassed to ask. She knew Sheila would have jumped at the offer, in any case. "Come on. No details?"

Sheila grinned. "Night of my life, Deb," she said lecherously. "I'm just hoping for another. I don't want to jinx it by kissing and telling."

He's happy enough to have sex with her, just not to stand up for her, Debbie thought. *So much for the romantic vampire.* "So how's the script?"

"Pretty great, actually," Sheila replied. "I'm more than half done and completely enthralled. I think it's the story of Dev's life." She looked down at the pages. "If more than half of this is true, he's done some amazing things." She grinned widely. "But it's not a straight romance like I expected, though it has some beautiful moments. It's got fights, suspense, evil villains, supernatural creatures, and damsels in distress. In short, all the makings of a great film."

Shaker was right about that vampire's appeal to women. "Good," Debbie said. "I worried it was going to need a lot of work. What's the title?"

"*Immortal Confessions*," Sheila said with a flourish. "It's perfect."

Debbie bit back an innuendo. Sheila might have enjoyed Dev, but she'd never judge a script with anything but a critical eye. "Sounds good to me. Let me know the details when you get a chance, and we'll get cracking on it."

Sheila nodded, then went back to reading.

Debbie walked back to her office. Song was waiting for her, oddly dressed up in a suit instead of her usual casual attire.

"Hi," Debbie said, looking her over head to toe.

"Hello," Song said meekly. She handed Debbie a form of several pages. "I was hoping you could cosign for me. I didn't want to ask Sheila."

Debbie looked it over. The loan paperwork was only for a few thousand dollars. "You're taking over the Black Rose?"

"Harp and I, yes," Song responded. "My brother got him—the owner, I mean—to sign it over to us before Harp killed him. I wanted to make a few improvements, before we opened." She beamed at Debbie. "You will always be welcome at no cost, of course."

Would Sheila ever join her again, though? It wouldn't be half so much fun going alone. "Has she talked to you about what happened?"

142

Debbie asked Song, as she scrawled her signature on the line.

"She was upset all last week," Song replied, whispering. "But she's coping. I feel awful, and I don't know what to do. Harp got all the bloody vengeance himself, without me." She looked at her small hands. "How do you make up something like this to someone?"

How did I get the role of demon counselor? Debbie thought. "Look, there is something you could do," she said to Song. "New Year's and Christmas are coming up, and we really need something smoking hot to celebrate Pandora's first year. Shaker proposed something about The Year of the Demon, but I haven't had any time to work on it, and I know Sheila hasn't either. Can you take that on for us? Shaker said he could call in a few favors, but we need some really original ideas—"

Song's smile was so wide Debbie worried her face would split open. "Of course!" she exclaimed. "I can already think of some good decorations. I'd love to do this for both of you!"

"Great," Debbie said happily. "See me if you need any money after Shaker gives you his connections to ask for favors. We need it for New Year's Eve, about seven to midnight, and to have enough refreshments on hand for all Pandora's employees."

Song had produced a pen and paper from somewhere and was writing it all down in shorthand, or some demon written language that resembled shorthand. "I'll take care of it," she said brightly. "You can rely on me, Mistress." She clapped a hand over her mouth, blushing. "Sorry. I meant Debbie." Song disappeared.

The intercom on Debbie's desk buzzed. "Ms. Deal?"

Debbie crossed to the desk. "Yes?"

"Henry Castle is here to see you. He says it's urgent."

Groan. "Please show him in."

Debbie sat down at her desk, and Henry came in the door, his expression grim. "What is this?" he said, tossing the paper she'd signed to request the return of some of his powers as her legal advocate down on her desk.

"My lawyer advised me to sign that," Debbie said evenly. "He said what you have been doing was going to leave us wide open for a takeover by Titan."

"Don't you trust me?" Henry said, hurt. "I've taken you through this every step of the way, Deb."

"I want to trust you," Debbie said, letting some of her angst into her tone. "But this isn't just me, Henry. This is Pandora. What kind of president would I be if I went against my legal counsel?"

"Then your legal counsel is steering you wrong," Henry replied. "Are you sure that he doesn't have his own agenda?"

Yes, Shaker said in Debbie's mind. *Catarella can be trusted implicitly.*

Where have you been? Debbie thought back at him. *Come to me immediately.*

I can't, Shaker said. *But I'll be there tonight at your house, okay?*

Okay, Debbie thought in relief. She raised her head to look at Henry. "I trust my counsel. Go ahead with the stock deal. If I have to pay more, that's worth it to me."

"You don't trust me," Henry said angrily.

"I trust you," Debbie said. "And when this deal goes through just like you planned, you can tell me I told you so." She smiled.

Henry shook his head, then walked out of her office. "It's your check to write. You want to pay through the nose, then go ahead."

Men, Debbie thought irritably. *They're worse than demons.*

* * * *

That night, Debbie waited for Shaker, nervously sipping a glass of wine. She finished it in record time, started to pour another, then put the bottle back, then grabbed it and poured another glass. *Why are you so nervous? It's just Shaker. So what if he looks different now?*

Debbie crossed to the window, and peered out. To her surprise, "Jett" was there at the curb, locking a sleek sports car, and then collecting some flowers and a bottle of wine before he strode up her walkway.

Debbie hurried to the door, unlocking it just as he was about to knock.

"Hi," Shaker said in Jett's voice. He looked her up and down. "You look lovely, Mistress."

"Why didn't you teleport?" Debbie asked, as she locked the door.

"It's much harder, when you're possessing someone." Shaker

144

handed the bottle of wine and flowers to Debbie. "For you."

"Thanks," Debbie said awkwardly. She sniffed the roses. "They're beautiful."

"Jett does have his uses," Shaker replied. "Now that he's not doing coke every night or buying prostitutes, he's debt-free and solvent." He grinned at Debbie.

"I'm glad he's reformed," Debbie stated drolly. "But how long will that last, once you leave him?"

"That is the holy wafer in the strawberry KY-gel, I'm afraid," Shaker said with a grimace. "Dear Jett will not be able to come back, Mistress. He's gone insane in the short time we've been together. So if you do want him to continue as your star, I will have to stay joined to him."

As bad news went, that...wasn't. Debbie smiled at Shaker. "Then stay joined. I take it you've been having fun as Jett? You haven't been around much lately."

"This is one of those things I'd rather you didn't ask," Shaker said in cool tones. "Trust me. I wasn't having fun. But I do have to tell you that possessing someone takes a lot of energy. I'm going to need another favor from you for a Christmas present."

"All right," Debbie said, after a moment. "I'll give you one by the weekend."

"By Christmas is soon enough," Shaker rumbled. "What did you make for dinner? I'm starved."

Debbie gaped at him.

"This human body needs to eat and do its other functions constantly," Shaker said with a chuckle. "I admit, it's fun to eat some of the foods available now that I never tried before. But I'm sick of needing to sleep, even if I do find the human male kind of dreaming enjoyable."

Debbie laughed herself at the delight in his tone. "With this kind of notice, I can make you...some spaghetti from a jar. Will that do?"

"Sounds good," Shaker replied. "I've not tried that yet. That's the long noodles in sauce, right?"

Debbie laughed, then began getting out the pot and filling it with water.

* * * *

"That was great," Shaker said, as he helped Debbie clean up the table.

"It was passable," Debbie corrected with a laugh. She put the empty bottle of wine in the trash, then turned to him with a sexy smile. "Should we open another?"

"I'm afraid I have to go," Shaker said apologetically.

Debbie gaped at him again, then flushed. She turned away, calling herself stupid for asking. *He probably had someone waiting for him back at his estate.*

"Just the maid," Shaker said gently, coming up behind Debbie and hugging her. "And she's sixty and married, Mistress."

Don't you want me anymore? Debbie thought the words she couldn't bring herself to utter.

"As much as always," Shaker whispered, kissing her ear. "Which is why I can't stay." He kissed her cheek, then walked to the door. Before Debbie could call out to him, he was gone.

* * * *

The next few weeks leading up to Christmas were a flurry of excitement, meetings, and preparation for the New Year's party. Song had gone into overdrive; every weekday there was a new note from her on Debbie's desk, telling her of additional plans. So far, she hadn't needed any cash funds, which was remarkable in Debbie's estimation.

Work on *Immortal Confessions* continued to go forward. Sheila had lined up everything but the score, which she told Debbie that Devlin himself was composing. Debbie groaned inwardly, but had to admit that so far the picture was looking good, at least on paper.

All the other pictures were also wrapping up nicely, too. *Smoke and Ashes II: Out of the Ashes* was already shooting, and Shaker had been busy working eleven-hour days as Jett. So far, that picture was on budget. *Absolution* was also shooting, although some scenes would have to wait until spring to be shot on location for the romantic ending. But that picture was also under budget. In fact, the only real problem Pandora currently faced was the werewolf turned weresnake picture that had

146

turned into the mess that Debbie had been sure Devlin's vampire picture would be. Lash had vetoed all three proposed scripts, and even stabbed one he particularly hated with his bowie knife. Sheila had one more left to show him, but she was at her wit's end. "He's unstable," she'd told Debbie over lunch. "He says that the special effects have to be 'realistic.' I told him we'd be able to use computers for that. He got angrier."

"Why?" Debbie had asked.

"He said, and I quote, 'I don't want to see some poof walking around fully dressed, then a flash and suddenly he's a snake flying through the air. It doesn't work like that for us. We're not making a fucking movie about furballs. Reptiles need to be shown to have some fucking class.'"

Debbie shook her head, laughing. "He's a piece of work, Lash is."

"I agree," Sheila said. She handed a booklet to Debbie. "Which is why you can show him this last script. I'm done with him hissing and brandishing his knife at me."

"I don't want to meet with him," Debbie retorted, pushing the paper back at Sheila. "Besides, I have to meet with Henry—"

"Not until Saturday, for preparation for that stock deal next week," Sheila interrupted, pushing the booklet right back. "Sorry, you have to do it, because I'm not."

Debbie grumbled, taking the booklet. Sheila grinned winningly, then walked out. And now it was close to five o'clock on Friday and Lash was due at any moment.

"Ms. Deal?" Kaitlin said, opening the office door a crack. "There's a Mr. Lash here to see you."

"Send him in," Debbie said wearily, pasting a smile on her face. "You can go on home, if you want to. Have a good week off, Kaitlin. Merry Christmas."

"Merry Christmas, Debbie," her secretary replied with a smile. She opened the door, then stepped away. "Go right in."

Lash swaggered in the door, then sat in the chair opposite Debbie's desk. "I hope you've got something good this time for me."

Debbie handed the script to him. "Take a look."

Lash read the first page, then tossed it down on the desk in disdain. "This sucks!"

Debbie held onto her smile with effort. "It's a werewolf story, I know, but we can modify it—"

"This guy's mooning over some babe," Lash hissed in disgust. "Why are all the scripts about some lonely wereman wanting to hang his shingle on the first human piece of ass to come along? Every werecreature I ever knew, that was the last thing on their minds!"

"This is a movie for humans, not for weremen, um, werecreatures," Debbie said patiently. "Humans going to see a movie want to see some romance. Remember your audience, Lash. Teen girls."

"Why does it have to be teen girls?" Lash hissed plaintively. "Can't I make a movie for men?"

"Men see movies like *Clear and Present Danger*, or *Fight Club*," Debbie said, wanting to strangle him. "They usually don't see movies about werecreatures. Consider also that those movies I mentioned were made for a broad audience, not men only. If you only target a small cross section of people, and they don't see the movie, then it probably will tank."

"Fuck," Lash said. He rubbed at his temples in obvious frustration, then looked up at her. "Say I wanted to make a movie like those two you mentioned for men. Can't we get a script like that and just insert a weresnake as the hero? Yeah, we might have to tweak it a little, but—"

"Look, Lash," Debbie said, her impatience getting the better of her. "Honestly, I don't think we are going to find you a script you're going to like. Weresnakes are still unknown." She forced another smile. "I didn't know such a thing existed before meeting you."

Lash stared at her, unmoving, his eyes shifting slightly to snake.

Was he going to whip out his knife? "Now," Debbie began nervously, "we can try to—"

The door crashed open, a looming horned figure in the doorway.

Go for the gun Mistress! Shaker bellowed in Debbie's head.

Lash snaked out of the chair so fast, he was turned and was facing the figure with his knife out before its second step. The monster was a dragon-like demon with long curving horns. Covered in scaly patches, its trident tail whipped back and forth angrily as it faced Lash. Then it looked past him to Debbie, uttering a maliciously happy hiss as it bared its long stained fangs.

148

"You fuck with me, you'll regret it," Lash hissed, assuming a fighting stance.

The monster weaved back and forth, then made to dart past him. Lash blocked it easily, and the thing opened its mouth, snarling in fury. Debbie crouched down behind her desk, feeling for the gun in the desk drawer. Her desperate hands touched only paper. *Someone took it!*

There was a loud crash, a grunt of pain, and then the monster peered over the desk at Debbie, it's lidded saucer eyes glowing green fire.

Debbie grabbed for her purse, going for the throwing stars as the demon grabbed hold of her left leg. She kicked hard, connected with a glancing blow, then shoved her hand into her purse, coming up with one of the stars as the thing grasped her leg, its talons digging in. The demon lifted her up, bringing her in close to its gaping mouth of spiked teeth.

Debbie yelled, then pushed the star into one of the saucer eyes as it made to bite into her arm. The thing shrieked, dropping her and clawing at its eye, black smoke curling up from the wound. Debbie crawled under the desk, the other two stars clenched in her hands.

There was an angry hiss, then a wet thunk. The demon screamed again. Next came a series of wet ripping sounds, then a hissing like steam. Debbie peered out from under the desk as the last clouds of black smoke dissipated, revealing Lash crouched on the floor, his hands and knife covered in black ichor. More of it spotted his face. He looked up at her.

"Got a towel?"

Debbie hurried out her office door to the bathroom right outside, and grabbed a fistful of the paper towels from the wall dispenser. She wet them in warm water, then hurried back, offering them to Lash. He took them, cleaning his knife first, then his hands. He tossed the used towels in her trash, then sat back down. "So what were you saying we should try?"

He's killed a demon, and now it's back to the movie? Damn, why hadn't Shaker suggested Lash as a solution? Debbie shifted in her chair. "Look," she started again. "Maybe we've been going about this all wrong." *Say it, even though you know it'll be a disaster.* "Maybe you should pen the script."

"What?" Lash said in surprise. "I don't know anything about making a screenplay. I've read plays, but only stuff like Macbeth."

"You don't have to write the screenplay," Debbie replied. "Just write the story the movie should be based on. Who better can tell the story of a weresnake than someone who is one?"

"Hmm," Lash said, sounding for all the world like Shaker that night he'd peered into Jett's boxer shorts. Debbie cleared her throat, blanking her mind of the image before she snorted and burst out laughing.

"But what do I write?" Lash asked again. "You said I had to worry about the audience. How the hell do I know what humans want in their stories?"

"Look at some of the more popular books and movies," Debbie offered. "Stories of redemption are always a big hit. Audiences like to root for the underdog. And if you're targeting males—like the action movies I mentioned—there need to be some fight scenes throughout the story with a bad guy and a really big one at the end, and at least one sexy female who comes across at some point for the hero, if you know what I mean."

"Of course," Lash said with a smirk. "I can include a slut or two. God knows I've known enough of them in my life." He stood up. "I'll try to write up something this week, and get it to you by New Year's. Will that work?"

Debbie considered telling him not to rush, that scripts often took years to create. But Sheila could deal with that, especially the extra fun part of adapting whatever dreck Lash wrote into some sort of workable screenplay. "Sounds good." She offered her hand. "Thank you for saving me for the second time, by the way."

"You're welcome," Lash said quietly. He considered her a moment. "You better make me a kick ass movie, Debbie Deal. I usually charge 100K for fighting a demon of Azaroth's level, minimum."

Dante's demon. The bastard had cracked and attacked directly, just like Shaker had said he would. Then Debbie realized what Lash had said. *100K was twice the budget of Absolution, and more than her yearly salary at Pandora. When he'd said he had money, he hadn't been kidding.* "Who are you?" Debbie stammered. "Even Shaker didn't want to take him on."

"I'm a Ranked assassin, is what I am," Lash answered, heading for the office door. "That's "Ranked" with a capital R, Debs. And I already have more than a few demons who count me their enemy. One more won't make a real difference. But no more freebies. Next time I'm sending you a bill in the mail."

"Does that mean Azaroth is dead?" Debbie yelled, hurrying after him. "Um, I mean that he won't be coming back again?"

Lash turned. "Ask your demon," he said with a crooked smile. "I'll be in touch."

Debbie went after him, but Lash had disappeared again. *Damn, if he can teleport, he must be part demon.* She righted her unneeded chairs, pulled a throw rug over the black stain on the carpet, gathered her things, and headed home.

After Debbie showered and dressed that night, she sat on her couch, thinking about everything. Lash had saved her ass. The gun was gone; someone had to have stolen it. But even if it had been there, it wouldn't have stopped the demon. She'd have been killed. Shaker had given her only the one command, then nothing. Maybe something had happened to him...

I'm outside, Mistress, Shaker said in her mind. *Let me in.*

Debbie went to the front door, relieved. "Jett" was there, his sports car behind him, dressed in ripped jeans and a battered jacket. She let him in, hanging up his jacket. "I think this is a little over-distressed," she said, as she hung it up. "It's practically a shredded rag."

"It was part of my costume for today's last scene," Shaker said, pouring himself some wine. "And back at five o'clock, it was pristine, like my jeans. And then all Hell broke loose." He grinned at her, but the smile didn't reach his eyes.

Debbie went over to him. What she had taken for a pattern on his shirt were bloodstains near each shoulder. His jeans were ripped, and one leg was torn badly, mud and blood at the edges of the tear. "What happened?"

"I killed him for you," Shaker answered. "Dante's dead."

"How? You said you didn't want to attack directly—"

"I saw the demon come for you," Shaker said. "I knew you'd have no chance to best him, even with the gun. There was no time to bring in the police like I planned. I teleported to Dante's house." He paused. "He wasn't alone."

Debbie touched his shoulder. "Who was there? What happened?"

"He'd bonded two demons, like Sheila," Shaker replied. "The other was low level, and didn't put up much of a fight. But getting him out of the way gave Dante long enough to get to his gun. He'd had the bullets blessed." He gave Debbie a shark's grin. "Lucky for me the fucker hadn't ever practiced with it, after stealing it from your office. He only managed to wing me twice."

Debbie took the glass away from Shaker, then began to undo his jeans.

"I knew fighting turned you on," Shaker said teasingly.

"Strip," Debbie said, pushing down the jeans, and then guiding Shaker to sit down in the nearest chair. "I'll throw these away. But I want to look at your wounds. We should put something on them."

"They're mostly healed up," Shaker said, even as he began taking off his clothes. "I've been gorging on meat the last few hours. They weren't bad, as I said, but the holy water causes severe pain, Mistress…which is why I shut down our mental link."

Debbie looked over his body. There were lighter scars on his shoulders, but he was right, the bullet holes were gone, leaving just a dark red area that looked like a bad burn. She touched the edge of one gently. "Does it still hurt?"

"You'd know if it did," Shaker said, looking at Debbie, then away. "You'd feel my pain."

They'd won. Why wasn't he happier? "What happens now?" Debbie asked, taking Shaker's hand in both of hers.

"Pandora is yours," Shaker said. "Or will be, once the paperwork is all straightened out."

"How?" Debbie asked, confused. "The stock deal isn't 'til next week."

"You don't need those shares anymore," Shaker said with surety. "You have Dante's shares."

"How in hell did you manage that?" Debbie echoed.

"With a little help from Hell," Shaker answered humorously. "Dante is going to be found tonight, if he hasn't been already. But he's not going to look like Dante anymore; he's going to be thought to be Paul. I cast an aging spell on him before I killed him. After he was dead, I dropped Jett's body and entered his, then used Dante's digital camera to make a video. In it Paul confesses how he's been kept a prisoner by his son for many months, and that his son is planning to kill him tomorrow."

"Why would anyone believe that?" Debbie said skeptically. "What about fingerprints? Motive? And why now, right before the stock deal went through?"

"The motive was Paul changing his will to exclude his son, and leaving everything to his wife. When Dante was told last New Year, he went insane and kidnapped his father. As to why kill off Paul now: Dante had been trying all this time to get his father to reconsider, so he could produce Paul and either stop Pandora going public, or make sure he got possession of all the shares going up for sale." Shaker reached for his wine, and took another sip. "No one is going to check fingerprints when they have all this other evidence. That is all for Hollywood stories, not for real police departments already stretched thin. When they see something that looks like an open and shut case, they'll be content to close it, especially with that detective O'Hara knowing Dante was dirty."

This is never going to work. "Thank you at least for killing Dante," Debbie said with fake cheer. "Just knowing I'm not going to be burned or demon food is enough right now."

"Don't be hasty," Shaker said slyly, drawing out the words. "The best stories are the ones that are partial truth, Mistress. That bit about Paul's new will is true. I found it in Dante's safe, after he literally spilled his guts. It was signed in late December of last year, probably when Paul and Rebecca were drawing up the deal with Titan. Dante had removed it from his father's safe after his father went missing. He had his demon kill the lawyer who made it and burn his office to cover his trail, so only the new will would be found and he could inherit the shares."

This tangle was more complex than an HBO drama series. "Why not destroy the will? If it ever was found—"

"He likely felt guilty about what he did," Shaker theorized. "And he didn't know his father was dead, though he should have. That low level demon he'd summoned out of hell was what used to be Paul." He drank the rest of his wine.

Debbie felt slight guilt over being responsible for Paul's death twice now, then pushed it down, irritated. "How could Dante not have known that was his own father?"

"Cursing sometimes leads to severe memory loss," Shaker supplied. "Take Rack, for example. It took him close to forty years to remember who he used to be. And if Paul was anything like his son, his mind might have just crumbled because he was weak. What I sent back to Hell was more animal than man."

Paul had always been base. "At least he'll have Dante to talk to."

"To torture, most likely," Shaker replied. "An apt punishment, I think."

Debbie moved to the window, a kind of peace descending on her. *It was finally over. Dante would never bother her again.* Snow was falling lightly, coating everything in white. "You should move your car inside, off the street. There's room in the garage."

"And what about for me?" Shaker said. Instead of his usual teasing tone, his voice was utterly serious.

"Can you stay tonight?" Debbie asked, turning to face him. "You didn't want to last time."

Shaker came over to her and hugged her, lips moving gently over her throat. "I wanted to stay the other night, Mistress. Believe me, it wasn't my choice to leave."

Debbie sighed, closing her eyes to luxuriate in the touch of his lips on her warm skin. "Then why did you?"

"If I stayed, you'd have made advances," Shaker whispered. "And I knew I wouldn't resist them." He moved back from her. "Jett was a drug user, Mistress. He might have hid it well, but…he was sick, Mistress. I didn't want you to catch what he had."

STDs? Debbie thought.

"Several," Shaker murmured. "I saw it that night I undressed in front of you. And also hepatitis, I'm afraid. I've been in treatment the last month getting rid of it."

Debbie moved back slightly, trying to keep the distaste off her face. "Are you better?"

"Much," Shaker whispered, kissing her ear.

Sorry, but the mood is going to take a little more time to recapture, Shaker. "Why didn't you tell me about Lash's fighting prowess?"

Debbie said. "He killed Dante's demon."

"Sent it to Hell," Shaker corrected. "I kind of have to feel sorry for Azaroth. He's always getting summoned by boys out for power. He's back in Hell almost before he's left."

"Why didn't you tell me about Lash being willing to fight demons?" Debbie repeated.

"Because you couldn't afford him," Shaker replied. He looked at her, worried. "Did he ask for a fee for defending you?"

"He said he would next time," Debbie answered. "And I have to make him his weresnake movie. Ugh."

"We got off easy, then," Shaker said, content. He pulled Debbie down on his lap, holding her.

"There are a lot of demons," Debbie mused, playing with a lock of Jett's black hair. "So there must be more like Lash, who hunt them for profit?"

"A few," Shaker admitted. "But I didn't mention them as a solution because we couldn't trust them, Mistress. They would kill you as soon as Dante. Anyone who has a demon is fair game to a demon hunter. I wasn't about to risk you. Remember Cahill?"

I do indeed. Point taken. "Are you hungry?" Debbie asked.

Shaker picked her up in his arms. "I'm famished for you, Mistress. Come with me, and let's test the limits of this body with yours."

"Are you sure you're up for it?" Debbie teased.

"All too sure," Shaker said lustily, carrying her toward the bedroom.

* * * *

Debbie stretched, then clasped Jett's body to her, luxuriating in his muscular arms. *Shaker's body*, she reminded herself mentally. *This was going to take some getting used to.*

Shaker stretched, emitting a happy groan.

"I'd say that was a complete trial run," Debbie uttered, sated.

"Yes," Shaker said, hugging her. "Lightbringer, but this feels good."

"It does," Debbie said happily. "I missed you a lot, Shaker."

"Enough to let me move in?" Shaker asked, smiling down at her

Debbie looked up at him, unsure of what to say, and trying to think of blank space so he wouldn't read her thoughts. *How could she decide anything without thinking about it? Argh!*

"If you want Henry, I'm not going to stand in the way," Shaker said. "But you asked me once what we can have. This body I possess gives us a way to be more, if you want to be."

"What do you want?" Debbie asked.

"I want to move in, obviously," Shaker said grumpily. "Or I wouldn't be asking."

"Pretty tawdry," Debbie proclaimed, even as she enjoyed the naughty feeling knowing the kind of gossip being Jett's girl publicly would cause. "The president of the company having one of her stars as a boy toy?"

"You are a little older than this body," Shaker said with a laugh. "I hadn't thought of that."

"Thanks," Debbie said sarcastically. "And it would help me, by the way, if you started referring to Jett's body as your body. I don't like to think I'm fucking some kind of zombie. Tawdry I can handle, but ghoulish and tawdry leaves me clammy."

"I never said it had to be tawdry," Shaker said, aloof. "I'll marry you as Jett, if you want."

Debbie stared at him, surprised. *Do you love me after all?*

"I want you to be happy," Shaker said carefully. "I think we could be. We understand each other, the way Triss and Rack do. They seem very happy together."

The new Triss, or the old one? "How much of this is the security of having a new host waiting in the wings?" Debbie said, biting her lip.

"None, unless you want to," Shaker assured. "I used protection last night, as you saw. But you're right that with me as Jett, we can have a family, if you want one." He kissed her hand gently. "Would you like that? You've never acted as if anything was important except Pandora."

Debbie remained silent.

Shaker kissed her forehead. "Think about it," he said. "It's an open-ended offer."

"Give me some time?" Debbie said suddenly. "With no peeking into my mind?"

"Of course," Shaker said. "Though I hope you'll excuse if I catch bits and pieces, when I check in with you periodically. It's kind of unavoidable."

Unsure how to answer, Debbie went into the kitchen. "I'll make us breakfast. Pancakes okay?"

"And bacon," Shaker called back. "I could really use some bacon, Mistress. Several packages, if you have them."

As she opened up the package of bacon, the doorbell rang.

Debbie went to the door, trying to remember if there was extra bacon in the downstairs freezer. This had to be UPS, with those last minute gifts she'd ordered to surprise Sheila: a set of weights and a workout bench. *God, it's only about nine am.* But Christmas was tomorrow night.

Debbie opened the door with a fake smile. "Please bring it...uh—"

Henry stood there, staring at her. "You weren't at the meeting," he said. "When you didn't answer your phone, I thought you were sick, so I came over."

"She was busy," Shaker said from behind her. For the first time, Debbie noted possessiveness in his voice, along with jealousy.

"You bitch," Henry said angrily, glaring at Debbie. "After all your bullshit about chastity."

Responses flashed through Debbie's mind, some witty, some cruel. She stayed silent, not wanting to make things worse.

Shaker put his arm around Debbie. "Please leave, Henry," he said firmly. "If Debbie wants to see you, she'll contact you."

"I loved you," Henry said, hurt. He looked with hate at Shaker. "You don't love her enough. You're just a beach bum addict looking for a way to save your sinking career."

For a split second, Debbie felt Shaker's anger swell, then his rapid-fire thoughts. *I've been her lover all along, stupid. You may love her, but you don't know her at all. You don't know what she wants, or what she's been through, but I do. And I'm not letting you fuck—*

The thoughts abruptly cut off, the feeling of anger evaporating.

"Debbie," Henry began. "Don't throw what we have away—"

Debbie looked at him, then down at the ring on her finger. Reluctantly, she removed the ring and handed it back to him. "I'm sorry, Henry. Please believe I never meant to hurt you." She looked up at him, suddenly blinking back tears. "But he's right. Please leave."

Henry pocketed the ring, then gave Debbie and Shaker one last hateful look. "You're going to regret this." Then he walked back to his car, started it, and roared away.

"Damn it," Debbie said, sniffling. "How could I have forgotten that stupid meeting this morning?"

Shaker hugged her, then brought her inside, locking the door. "Because it wasn't important, Mistress." He kissed her cheek. "Forget him, at least for now. There will be time enough to deal with Henry at some later date."

Debbie didn't answer, moving to the cupboard.

Shaker went with her. "For what it's worth," he whispered. "Catarella was right. Henry was planning on selling you out to Titan."

"How do you know?" Debbie said, biting her lip.

"I saw it in his mind just now," Shaker replied. "Images of what he'd hoped for. Titan would have acquired Pandora, you'd have been given a large raise and retained your role as president, and Henry would have gotten you."

"Why?" Debbie whispered.

"He wanted it all, like most humans," Shaker said, hugging her. "Desire for perfection is the most common failing of your species, Mistress."

Standing there in Shaker's arms, Debbie suddenly felt alone and afraid. *Henry hadn't been perfect, but he'd been human at least. She'd known the emotions that drove him. Could she ever say the same of Shaker, no matter how human he looked now?*

"Mistress—"

"You said you needed a favor," Debbie said tiredly. "Choose someone in Europe. I leave it to you. Do it as soon as possible."

"Yes, Mistress," Shaker murmured.

* * * *

"Merry Christmas," Sheila said happily, walking in Debbie's door. A Santa hat was on her head, slightly off-center.

"Ow," Song said plaintively, looking disgruntled as she followed Sheila inside.

"Sorry," Sheila said. "I meant Happy Yule."

158

"How many times do we have to tell you, that's still a faith," Harp griped, setting down a large chocolate gift basket under Debbie's tree.

"I hope the decorations don't bother you?" Debbie said to the demons. "Shaker hasn't mentioned anything."

"He doesn't get bothered," Song said nastily. "Original fallen angel, and all that crap. But we're second generation, and let me tell you, it hurts."

"You two have to grow a thicker skin," Shaker said, appearing as Jett. "Christmas means Santa and presents and commercialism nowadays. Faith is practically absent. Hell, it's not even Christ's real birthday—"

"OUCH," both Harp and Song chorused loudly.

Shaker rolled his eyes. "You're way too sensitive. But you didn't come for theology. Let's break out the alcohol. Sheila, what would you like?"

"Are you sure you should?" Song teased in singsong voice. "Your flesh suit is a reformed addict, after all."

"That I have well in hand," Shaker said loftily. "In point of fact, though, I think you should get used to calling me Jett."

Harp and Song gaped at him.

"It makes sense," Shaker continued. "You call me Shaker and someone overhears, they'll remember it."

"I'll have a bourbon on the rocks," Sheila said, sitting down. "So humanity is growing on you, Jett?"

"Having a life is growing on me," Shaker said with a grin, pouring her drink. "Here you go."

"Never thought I'd see the day," Harp said in mock sorrow. "Our fearless leader's turned human jock."

"There's a lot to be said for Jett," Debbie chimed in, handing drinks to Song and Harp. "I wouldn't have ever liked to be a wife." She sipped her own glass of wine. "Henry wanted to make me one. But I do want a partner and a friend. Shaker can be that, as Jett."

Song and Harp shared a glance.

"Sounds serious," Sheila quipped. "Is there a rock?"

Debbie busied herself in the kitchen, not sure how to answer, again worried her feelings would color her thoughts, and that Shaker would see

159

them.

"I'm moving in here," Shaker said, after a moment.

"Congratulations," Sheila said, to Debbie, raising her glass. "I hope you'll be very happy."

"You know he won't like it," Harp said to Shaker softly.

Shaker stopped still, his gaze locking with Harp's. "I know," he said just as softly. "But I'm doing it anyway."

Harp stared at him a moment more, then his face split into a grin. "Let's hear it for rebellion." He raised his glass. "Salut!"

The night passed enjoyably, the friends exchanging presents, laughing, and drinking. As the party wound down to the wee hours, Harp serenaded them on his harp of bones, playing hauntingly beautiful music. While he and his instrument were at odds with the decorations, Debbie enjoyed his moving music immensely. It had all the longing inside her, all her angst, and all her joy in this night contained in its unearthly melody. *I'm so happy...*

Debbie blinked her eyes, realizing she was being undressed. She flailed suddenly.

"It's just me," Shaker whispered, slipping off her socks. He crawled into bed beside her, holding her.

"Sorry," Debbie said. "I take it I fell asleep?"

"You and Sheila both," Shaker said. "That's normal. Harp's music has magic to it. I hope it gave you some good dreams."

"None I remember."

"Well, get some sleep," Shaker said gently. "You're getting a second chance at those good dreams."

Say it before you lose your nerve. "Shaker?"

"Hmm?"

"Who was Harp referring to? The person that wouldn't like you moving in here?"

There was a long pause. "You know," Shaker said finally in a low voice.

"I think I do," Debbie said slowly. "Your boss." *The devil.*

"Yes."

Why? Debbie thought to Shaker

I killed Dante.

160

I know that, Debbie replied, confused. *Why—?*

I killed him before Lash killed Azaroth, Shaker admitted. *That's why Lash didn't charge you. He's a professional. He never kills for free. And because he didn't charge you, that means he knows he didn't deliver Azaroth's death blow.*

What does that mean for us?

Maybe nothing, Shaker replied. *Lash is no friend to demons. Dante and Azaroth exited within a minute of one another, so if we're lucky, no one will know the truth.*

But if no one knows, why are you so worried, Shaker?

Because of that revenant you told me about. Dante did not admit to sending it after you, and he admitted everything else. I should have questioned him longer, but you were in danger, and—

Shaker's thoughts were laced with deep worry, enough to make Debbie feel a flicker of doubt, even as she tried to reassure him. *It's okay.*

He didn't reply.

Shaker?

The truth is...I'm worried because this is as close to happy as I can probably get, he answered sadly. *And that's not...encouraged, you might say.*

I'm sorry. Debbie hugged him tightly

Shaker hugged her back, and didn't answer.

Epilogue

~ New Years Eve ~

"You've outdone yourself," Debbie said to Song, who smiled proudly.

The large conference room was decked with black and red ribbons and elaborate banners with silhouettes of demons in red foil on a black border. Scattered braziers burned, sweet incense filling the air. Life-size cardboard statues of various Pandora heroes and villains stood here and there. The nearest one was Jett Black, as Storm of *Smoke and Ashes*. Debbie looked at him with delight, imagining his skin pressed against hers. *Later on, it will be…*

"It does look beautiful," Sheila said. "Who is the band?"

"Some local talent," Song said nervously. "But they play covers. I picked songs with demon references."

As if on cue, the band began playing, the lively tones of "Sympathy for the Devil" filling the room.

"I have spectacularly good news," Sheila gushed to Debbie and Song. "I had to tell you first though, before I announce it."

"You're becoming a vampire?" Debbie said with wide eyes.

"Jerk," Sheila said, flashing Debbie a hurt look.

"Sorry," Debbie said contritely. "Please tell me."

"Smoke and Ashes production costs were close to $2 million; worldwide marketing doubled that, and a third of the proceeds went to theaters and distributors. You knew it was over budget; I know that's not

162

a surprise—"

"But?" Debbie prodded.

"But it grossed 4 million already!" Sheila said excitedly. "And that's just for opening weekend! It's one of the biggest openings for an independent picture, ever!"

Debbie hugged her tightly. "That is wonderful news," she gushed. "Pandora couldn't have done it without you, Sheila."

"Or without you," Sheila whispered. She kissed Debbie's cheek discreetly, then released her.

"I think you're both to be congratulated," a melodious voice said. Debbie and Sheila turned to see Devlin, resplendent in a bright red leather suit and pants, and a white silk shirt. "Your pardon, but it was impossible not to overhear the good news."

Only he could make that outfit work. "Thank you," Debbie said pleasantly.

"If I might take a moment to consult with you, in private?" Devlin inquired of Sheila. "I have some matters that urgently need your expert opinion." She nodded, then walked off with him.

"How much you want to bet she doesn't want our company tonight?" Song whispered to Harp, who grumbled something.

"I'll take that bet," Lash hissed from a few feet away. He was dressed as usual in black jeans and a black turtleneck with a black denim shirt. "Dev's a more-the-merrier kind of guy."

"Don't you ever wear anything else?" Song remarked, irritated. "This is an important party."

"Why don't you be a good little demon and fuck off?" Lash said pleasantly, walking closer. "I need to do some consulting of my own with Debbie."

Oh no. Sheila, you are so dead for leaving me here to deal with this. "What is it?" Debbie asked him.

Lash handed her a few pages. "I've only got as far as the first two chapters. But I'm worried that I'm...that the hero is not sympathetic enough."

God, the snakeman copied the vampire and wrote down his own life story...Say something, anything. Debbie took the pages. "What do you mean?"

163

"I mean that he's killing people," Lash replied, uncomfortable. "Do human audiences mind if the hero does that, if the people are clearly assholes that deserve it?"

"Most of the time, no," Debbie said, blinking rapidly. "As long as the man is provoked—"

"He's a ten year old boy, at the beginning," Lash interrupted. "Not a man. But he's very provoked."

Do not say anything that could be taken for a commitment. "Let me look at it and see," Debbie said vaguely. "I'll let you know."

"I want him to come across as a…well, as a person to root for, like that underdog you talked about," Lash said hopefully. "But I worry some people will see him as a villain, for the things he does. I need to know if he's sympathetic—"

Keep smiling. "I'll have Sheila take a look, and get back to you," Debbie said with false brightness. "She's the best one to tell if something is good or not. If she thinks audiences won't go for it, she's sure to be able to come up with some good recommendations for you."

"Good," Lash replied. He looked around, then headed off in the direction of the bar.

Debbie watched him go with an inward sigh of relief. Then she noticed that a new song had begun. The new Mrs. Triss and Rack were on the dance floor, both of them dressed in white and black. Debbie had to admit they did look happy together as they swept across the dance floor, their eyes locked on one another.

"I guess romance isn't dead," a nearby guest commented, watching the couple.

"…still I hunger for you when you look at me…"

Debbie had a mental flash suddenly of herself, surrounded by guests. She looked up to see Shaker watching her from across the room. *He had let her see through his eyes.*

"…that face, those eyes, all the sinful pleasures deep inside…"

His blue eyes suddenly flashed red, then faded back to blue as he gave her a sensual smile. Debbie smirked at him. He grinned back happily.

I didn't know the bond worked both ways, Debbie thought to Shaker. *That I could see through your eyes.*

I wanted you to see you as I see you, Mistress. You look very beautiful tonight.

Giorgio patted Debbie on the shoulder, breaking her concentration. "This is a great party, Debbie."

"I had a great team," Debbie said graciously. "Enjoy yourself tonight."

As Giorgio walked off, Debbie turned towards the music, trying to make out the words

"Tell me how you know now
the ways and means of getting in
underneath my skin
Oh, you were always my original sin."

You were, you know, Debbie thought to Shaker. *I never sinned so much in one year...or had so much fun, either. I know there were some bad times, but we really made a great team, even when times were bad. Sometimes it's hard to believe it was all real and not a dream.*

The year's not over yet, Mistress, he replied. *Meet me in your office at five of midnight.*

Debbie caught his gaze and nodded, then turned away.

* * * *

"This better be good," Debbie warned Shaker as he led her into her office. "I'm missing Sheila's big announcement of our record profits."

Shaker turned to her. "I thought we should begin the New Year the way we did the last one. It was a good year, as you said. We need to give thanks for that."

"Are you superstitious?" Debbie teased.

"Sometimes," Shaker answered. He opened a bottle of one of the Triss vintages, poured two glasses, and handed one to her. "To us. May the coming New Year be as good as the last one."

Debbie clinked glasses with Shaker, and drank. As she put down her glass, Shaker grabbed her hand, putting something small and hard into her palm. Debbie held it up to the light. It was a ruby ring, with black onyx on either side. The center stone shone with an inner fire, the side stones a dull inky black.

Debbie turned to Shaker. "What does this mean?"

165

"Whatever you want it to," he answered. "I know you liked the ring Henry gave you, and I wanted to get you something special."

It was now or never. "And if I said I wanted what he offered me, too?" Debbie managed.

"Then I'd accept, of course," Shaker said graciously. "It'd be bad manners to refuse—"

Debbie went to hit him, but he caught her, pulling her into his arms for a passionate kiss. *Shh*, he said tenderly. *You know I want you. You've known it for months now.*

Debbie smiled, even as she blinked away tears. *I want you, too.*

Good, he replied. *But we must be careful, Mistress. What we are doing is close to breaking a lot of rules. It would be better if anything with emotion was said like this, so that no one can possibly know but us.*

Debbie nodded.

"I thought you might choose Henry, that day at your house," Shaker murmured. "He did love you, Mistress."

He never had a chance, Debbie whispered mentally. *You'd already gotten underneath my skin. And the funny thing is when I look back at the year, I have no idea when it began.*

When you knew we could talk without speaking, Shaker replied. *I never misunderstand you, because I can feel everything you feel. You're never ignored, because I'm your sworn protector.* "You can hide very little from me, Debbie. That kind of closeness eventually breeds either affection, or contempt."

"I'm glad you don't find me contemptible," Debbie remarked with arched brows.

"Do you know how awful it is to have to be as close as we are with someone you loathe?" Shaker said with a grimace. He looked at her with affection. "You aren't the only one who is glad, Mistress."

"About that," Debbie said slowly. "We need to talk at some point. I want to set some new parameters for the New Year." *There's something I wanted to give you.*

Shaker looked at her, waiting.

I don't want things to go on as they have been between us, Debbie thought to him.

There was a flash of pain through the mental link, then it vanished.

I mean that I will still choose favors, Debbie explained hurriedly. *I don't want you to go back to Hell. But I don't want you to be my protector, or my avenger, or my slave anymore, either. I expect you to respect me, and to tell me the truth, but that's all.* She clasped his hand. *If you stay as Jett, I want you to stay because it's your choice, not mine.*

Shaker didn't say a word as he gazed at her. But there was a shifting, as of a veil lifting. Suddenly Debbie felt his profound gratefulness, his relief, his affection for her, and his happiness. He squeezed her hand. Then carefully he took her left hand in both of his, and slipped the ruby ring onto her finger. "I think we've said all we need to, my Mistress," he said huskily. "Come with me. Sheila's just ending her speech. Let's begin this New Year with a little announcement of our own."

Debbie nodded, blinking back happy tears that threatened to spill over. Together, she and Shaker hurried back to the party, arriving just as the first shouts of "Happy New Year!" rang out.

"To Pandora's great year!" Sheila said in closing, raising her glass at the front of the room. "And to an even better, stellar, New Year to come!"

Yes, Shaker murmured to Debbie, as his hand closed around hers. *It will be.*

About the Author

Tara Fox Hall's writing credits include nonfiction, horror, suspense, action-adventure, erotica, and contemporary and historical paranormal romance. She is the author of the paranormal action-adventure *Lash* series and the vampire romantic suspense *Promise Me* series. Tara divides her free time unequally between writing novels and short stories, chainsawing firewood, caring for stray animals, sewing cat and dog beds for donation to animal shelters, and target practice.

www.tarafoxhall.com

Other works by the author with Melange Books, LLC

Return To Me
Surrender to Me
The Origin of Fear in Spellbound 2011 Anthology
Night Music in Midnight Thirsts II Anthology
Partners in Midnight Thirsts II Anthology
Kink in Wicked Christmas Wishes Anthology
The Oath in Wicked Christmas Wishes Anthology
Bedtime Shadows Anthology
Make Me Behave Anthology
Latham's Landing, An Anthology
The Oath
Her Frozen Heart, in Frozen Anthology
Night Music, a Novella

The Promise Me Series
Promise Me, Book 1
Broken Promise, Book 2
Taken in the Night, Book 3
Taken for his Own, Book 4
Promise Me Anthology, Book 4.5
Immortal Confessions, Book 5
Her Secret, Book 6
Point of No Return, Book 7
Lost Paradise, Book 8
Dark Solace, Book 9
Eye of the Storm, Book 10
Tempest of Vengeance, Book 11

www.ingramcontent.com/pod-product-compliance
Lightning Source LLC
Chambersburg PA
CBHW030510260626
47157CB00005B/1725